"Can we get her a Christmas present?"

What did you get for a woman who must have everything?

"We'll get a poinsettia," Alex promised his son. Plants were usually safe, especially since it should look like a seasonal gesture.

Jeremy looked relieved, and turned his head to gaze in the direction Shannon had driven. For the first time in a year his son wasn't clutching Mr. Tibbles to his chest; instead, he was casually swinging the stuffed animal by one arm.

Alex sighed. He had to be careful. Seeing too much of the woman next door could lead Jeremy into getting ideas about a new mommy.

Yet Alex couldn't help thinking about Shannon. She was as different from his wife as a woman could be. He'd considered dating since Kim's death, but none of the women he'd met were particularly interesting.

And none of them were like Shannon O'Rourke.

Dear Reader,

What is the best gift you ever received? Chances are it came from a loved one and reflects to some degree the love you share. Or maybe the gift was something like a cruise or a trip to an exotic locale that raised the hope of finding romance and lasting love. Well, it's no different for this month's heroes and heroines, who will all receive special gifts that extend beyond the holiday season to provide a lifetime of happiness.

Karen Rose Smith starts off this month's offerings with *Twelfth Night Proposal* (#1794)—the final installment in the SHAKESPEARE IN LOVE continuity. Set during the holidays, the hero's love enables the plain-Jane heroine to become the glowing beauty she was always meant to be. In *The Dating Game* (#1795) by Shirley Jump, a package delivered to the wrong address lands the heroine on a reality dating show. Julianna Morris writes a memorable romance with *Meet Me under the Mistletoe* (#1796), in which the heroine ends up giving a widower the son he "lost" when his mother died. Finally, in Donna Clayton's stirring romance *Bound by Honor* (#1797), the heroine receives a "life present" when she saves the Native American hero's life.

When you're drawing up your New Year's resolutions, be sure to put reading Silhouette Romance right at the top. After all, it's the love these heroines discover that reminds us all of what truly matters most in life.

With all best wishes for the holidays and a happy and healthy 2006.

Ann Leslie Tuttle
Associate Senior Editor

Please address questions and book requests to:
Silhouette Reader Service
U.S.: 3010 Walden Ave., P.O. Box 1325, Buffalo, NY 14269
Canadian: P.O. Box 609, Fort Erie, Ont. L2A 5X3

Julianna Morris

MEET ME UNDER THE MISTLETOE

SILHOUETTE *Romance*®

Published by Silhouette Books

America's Publisher of Contemporary Romance

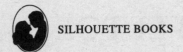 SILHOUETTE BOOKS

ISBN 0-373-19796-9

MEET ME UNDER THE MISTLETOE

Copyright © 2005 by Julianna Morris

This edition published by arrangement with Harlequin Books S.A.

® and TM are trademarks of Harlequin Books S.A., used under license. Trademarks indicated with ® are registered in the United States Patent and Trademark Office, the Canadian Trade Marks Office and in other countries.

Visit Silhouette Books at www.eHarlequin.com

Printed in U.S.A.

Books by Julianna Morris

Silhouette Romance

Baby Talk #1097
Family of Three #1178
Daddy Woke Up Married #1252
Dr. Dad #1278
The Marriage Stampede #1375
*Callie, Get Your Groom #1436
*Hannah Gets a Husband #1448
*Jodie's Mail-Order Man #1460
Meeting Megan Again #1502
Tick Tock Goes the Baby Clock #1531
Last Chance for Baby! #1565
†A Date with a Billionaire #1590
†The Right Twin for Him #1676
†The Bachelor Boss #1703
†Just Between Friends #1731
†Meet Me under the Mistletoe #1796

*Bridal Fever!
†Stories of the O'Rourke family

JULIANNA MORRIS

has an offbeat sense of humor, which frequently gets her into trouble. She is often accused of being curious about everything—her interests ranging from oceanography and photography to traveling, antiquing, walking on the beach and reading science fiction. Julianna loves cats of all shapes and sizes, and recently she was adopted by a feline companion named Merlin. Like his namesake, Merlin is an alchemist—she says he can transform the house into a disaster area in nothing flat.

Julianna happily reports meeting her Mr. Right. Together they are working on a new dream of building a shoreline home in the Great Lakes area.

THE O'ROURKE FAMILY TREE

Keenan (d) m. Pegeen

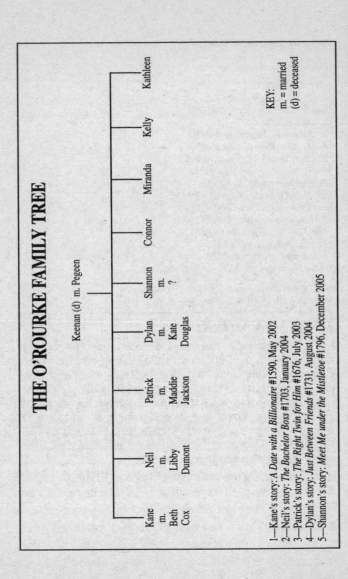

Kane
m.
Beth
Cox

Neil
m.
Libby
Dumont

Patrick
m.
Maddie
Jackson

Dylan
m.
Kate
Douglas

Shannon
m.
?

Connor

Miranda

Kelly

Kathleen

KEY:
m. = married
(d) = deceased

1—Kane's story: *A Date with a Billionaire* #1590, May 2002
2—Neil's story: *The Bachelor Boss* #1703, January 2004
3—Patrick's story: *The Right Twin for Him* #1676, July 2003
4—Dylan's story: *Just Between Friends* #1731, August 2004
5—Shannon's story: *Meet Me under the Mistletoe* #1796, December 2005

Chapter One

Shannon O'Rourke pulled into a spot in the post office parking lot and then grabbed her Christmas cards. Normally she would have mailed them at work, but she was reluctantly taking a few vacation days from her job as a public relations director.

In a nearby parking space she saw her new neighbor getting out of his Jeep Cherokee.

She'd only seen Alex McKenzie once, but according to the gossipy head of the condominium association, he was a thirty-four-year-old widowed college professor with a doctorate in engineering.

He was also one of the most ruggedly handsome men she'd ever seen.

"Jeremy, leave Mr. Tibbles in the Jeep for now," he said, unfastening a small boy from a child's booster seat.

The boy climbed down from the Jeep with his father's help, clutching a worn stuffed rabbit to his chest. He was a miniature version of Alex McKenzie, and warmth spread through Shannon's heart at the sight of the serious youngster, his blue eyes older and more worried than they should have been.

"It's okay, son, Mr. Tibbles won't mind staying behind this time," Dr. McKenzie urged.

Jeremy shook his head, holding the rabbit tighter.

His father sighed and passed a hand over the boy's dark brown hair. "All right. Stay here while I get the packages out of the car."

A few moments later he maneuvered his son and a large stack of boxes toward the front door of the post office. Shannon dashed after them.

"Dr. McKenzie...let me help," she called.

Alex turned and saw a flame-haired beauty hurrying toward him. There was something familiar about the woman, though he couldn't place her.

"Excuse me," he said, "do I know you?"

"I'm Shannon O'Rourke, your neighbor."

"Oh, right." Alex remembered the day the previous month when they'd moved into the condo from their apartment. He'd been talking to the movers when a woman had pulled into the next driveway, bundled in a heavy coat, with only her auburn hair visible. She'd waved her hand in a quick hello before rushing inside to escape the rain.

It was warmer today and she was dressed in designer jeans that showed off a pair of long legs, and a cashmere sweater that left no doubt about her slim waist and womanly curves. She exuded confidence and flashed an engaging smile.

One of the packages slipped from his grasp and Shannon caught it. "Let me have some of those," she said, taking several without waiting for agreement. She stepped around him and looked over her shoulder. "Coming?"

One of his eyebrows shot upward. *Shy* and *retiring* obviously weren't in the woman's vocabulary.

Alex took Jeremy's hand.

Everyone said the holidays were especially hard for a spouse who's lost a partner, but the toughest part for Alex was trying to make things right for his four-year-old son. This would be the first Christmas without his wife. Kim's death the past January had left a huge hole in their lives. No matter how good it might be, a day-care center couldn't take the place of a mother like Kim.

The thought of his wife made Alex ache. His friends had called him the most married man they knew, even though he'd spent so much time working out of the country. But they were right. He'd recognized what he had, a sweet, gentle woman who wouldn't tear him apart the way his parents had torn each other apart. You didn't find that kind of love twice.

Shannon nudged the door open with her hip and waited for father and son to go ahead of her.

"That's my job," Alex said, "opening a door for a lady. But I suppose you're one of those modern women who don't believe in that sort of thing."

Shannon opened her mouth, ready to toss out a smart remark, then hesitated. She'd always believed in being herself, and if a man didn't like it, then too bad.

But she wasn't sure what "being herself" was anymore.

She wanted more out of life. She wanted to be in love and married, but lately her love life was practically nonexistent. And now that four of her five brothers were happily wed, the desire to find love such as they had was even stronger. But her life seemed stuck in Neutral, while everyone else's was Full Speed Ahead.

"I don't mind," she said finally. It was true. She didn't object to men being chivalrous; she'd just learned that waiting for a guy to hold a door could get embarrassing.

"All right." Alex rested his shoulder against the door to hold it. "I've got it, then. Go ahead, Miss O'Rourke."

He was close enough for her to smell the faint scent of his aftershave, and Shannon's knees wobbled. That wasn't good. According to her three sisters, Kelly, Miranda and Kathleen, men with children were complicated, especially when it came to their motives toward women.

She glanced down at Jeremy's grave face. "Go 'head," he said, and she melted.

"Thank you," Shannon murmured.

She glanced swiftly at Alex in her peripheral vision, then walked toward the long line of people waiting for service. Her condominium was in a small bedroom community outside of Seattle, but the post office had the usual holiday crowd. It looked as though they'd be waiting for a while, something she was foolishly happy about.

Lord, she had to be crazy.

For Pete's sake, he'd called her *Miss* O'Rourke and said his job was holding the door for a lady. Alex McKenzie was obviously the same breed of old-fashioned guy as the male half of the O'Rourke family. She could spot the type a mile away, and usually ran the opposite direction. She'd dated one in college, only to get her heart broken when he'd dumped her, saying he wanted a homemaker like his mother…something she definitely *wasn't*. Her only talent in the kitchen was turning perfectly good food into inedible, blackened messes.

A tug at the hem of her sweater made her look down. It was Jeremy.

"I can help," he said, pointing at the packages she still carried.

"Oh…all right. May I hold Mr. Tibbles for you? He can sit on top of my purse while we wait."

Jeremy regarded her for a long moment.

Mr. Tibbles was plainly a very important stuffed rabbit not to be entrusted to just anyone. Shannon crouched so she could be eye-to-eye with the boy. Something about him reminded her of how she'd felt after losing her father when she was a child herself, and her heart throbbed with the old grief.

"I promise to take very good care of him." She smiled reassuringly.

After what seemed an eternity, Jeremy nodded and traded Mr. Tibbles for two of the packages. She settled the rabbit so its feet were anchored in her purse, and made sure it stayed in full view of its protective human. Only after the exchange had been completed did she see Alex's stunned expression.

"Is something wrong?" she asked.

"I don't know how you managed that. I haven't been able to separate him from that rabbit since his mother died," Alex said in a low voice. "He only lets go in the bath, and that's because he says Mr. Tibbles is afraid of the water. You must have a gift with children."

Shannon swallowed. What she knew about children could be written on the head of a pin. "Um…I like kids," she said tentatively.

It wasn't a lie.

Kids were great little people and she would love to have one someday. Her three nieces and one nephew were the most precious things in the world.

Alex's gaze was fixed on his son who had wandered over to the Christmas tree in the corner. There was so much pain in his eyes that Shannon's throat tightened. This was a man who'd lost his wife and was trying to raise his child alone. And it was Christmas, a time when absences were felt worse than ever. She remembered what it was like after her father died—nothing had been right, and even now there were moments when emptiness replaced holiday cheer.

"This time of year must be rough," she said softly.

"His mother made things so special for Christmas," Alex murmured, his gaze still focused on his son. "She loved baking and doing crafts with him, and fixing things just right. It's been hard trying to make up for what he's lost."

Shannon shifted her feet, feeling torn.

She couldn't get involved with a man grieving over his wife's death. It was simply asking for a broken heart. Besides, her relationships never lasted. Old-fashioned or not, the men she continually found herself dating inevitably wanted her to be less modern and more a domestic goddess in disguise.

Well, she didn't have an ounce of domesticity in her.

But what about Jeremy? He had responded to her, and that meant something. Didn't it?

"W-why is the rabbit so important to Jeremy?" Shannon asked, despite the internal warnings clanging inside her head. She could tell when a man wasn't interested, and Dr. McKenzie had disinterest written all over his face.

"I'm not sure." Alex gave her a crooked smile. "Maybe you can figure it out."

Shannon knew she should confess her ignorance about children. On the other hand, she did know about hurting.

Pain seemed bottled up inside Jeremy and it wasn't right; a child shouldn't have to go through so much.

"I'm sorry things have been so hard. Settling into a new place must make it harder," she murmured instead. "If there's anything I can do, please let me know." She swallowed an offer to babysit while she was on vacation.

"Thank you, Miss O'Rourke. That's kind of you," Alex said formally, in a tone that announced he had no intention of asking for anything.

She cocked her head. "Please call me Shannon. Nobody uses Miss O'Rourke unless they want to annoy me. Even reporters aren't that formal during a press conference."

"Do you talk to reporters very often?"

Shannon shrugged. "It's part of my job. I'm the Public Relations Director for O'Rourke Enterprises."

"Of course," he said. "You're one of the O'Rourkes."

Her nose wrinkled.

Terrific, she was one of the O'Rourkes. Her oldest brother was a talented businessman who'd made truckloads of money. As one of the richest men in the country, Kane had gotten more press than most movie stars, so people tended to recognize the name. Especially in the Seattle area.

"Sorry," Alex murmured, his lazy, comfortable grin sending her pulse skidding. It didn't make sense; he wasn't the type of man she usually dated. "You must get tired of people saying things like that."

"Now and then."

He cleared his throat and motioned to the line that had moved away from them. Shannon strolled forward, making sure that Mr. Tibbles remained within Jeremy's sight now that he'd rejoined them. The boy was so young. She wondered if he remembered his mother, or if it was the sense of abandonment that still haunted him. It was hard for a child to understand that their mommy or daddy hadn't wanted to die. But death wasn't a concept children understood very well.

Nor did some adults, Shannon reflected wryly.

There were times she heard her father's voice in her subconscious and turned around, half expecting to see him standing there.

She let out a breath and looked up at Alex. "I understand you teach engineering. My brother Kane wanted to be an engineer, but he had to quit school."

"Instead he became a billionaire," Alex said dryly. "It must be rough."

Shannon's eyes narrowed. She might complain about her atavistic brothers, but nobody criticized Kane except her. He'd done everything for the family, giving up his own plans for the future. The fact that he'd made a fortune in the process just proved his intelligence and determination.

"Kane is brilliant," she said in a cool tone. "Until he got married he worked fourteen hours a day, so he was hardly living a life of ease and luxury. Money was just his way of taking care of the family after we lost our father. He would have been a wonderful engineer, but he never got the chance."

The corners of Alex's mouth twitched. He'd never have believed the vibrant redhead was capable of looking so frosty. She might be fashion-model beautiful, but when it came to her precious brother, she was pure pit bull.

"I wasn't criticizing," he said.

"Of course you weren't."

She turned her back to him, and he sighed. Women like

Shannon O'Rourke were too volatile for a down-to-earth guy like him. And too unpredictable. He liked engineering schematics and formulas, things you could count on. Life was uncertain enough without inviting chaos into the mix.

The line had moved and they finally reached the front, where a postal clerk waited expectantly.

"Our turn," Jeremy said to Shannon.

She nodded. "You're such a big help. Let's put the packages on the counter, so your daddy can mail them." She cast a glance toward Alex. "And I'll mail my Christmas cards."

"Okay."

Jeremy handed up the packages, which Shannon piled on the counter along with the ones she'd carried. Almost as an afterthought, she added her bundle of Christmas cards, which Alex noticed were already stamped. She hadn't needed to wait in line with them.

"Well, Jeremy, I'd better return Mr. Tibbles to you, and then get going."

Shannon took the stuffed rabbit out of her purse and passed it to Jeremy, who didn't seem to hold it quite as fiercely as before. Alex rubbed his chin as he watched Shannon walk away. His son had never accepted someone so quickly. Hell, she'd gotten Mr. Tibbles away from him with just a smile—he hadn't managed that feat and he was Jeremy's father.

"It all goes first-class mail. I'll be back in a minute," he muttered to the postal clerk, shoving his credit card in her direction. Muffled groans of protest came from the waiting customers, but Alex ignored them. "Miss O'Rourke," he said, catching Shannon at the exit. "That is…Shannon."

"Ever the gentleman, Dr. McKenzie," she murmured. "But I can manage this door on my own."

"That wasn't what I meant."

"You mean you don't want to hold the door for me?" Shannon sounded offended and he groaned.

"No, that is, yes, of course I do, but…"

Too late he saw the faint humor lurking in her green eyes.

He'd been had, yet he wanted to laugh as well. There weren't many women who could forgive a supposed insult that quickly. Especially one concerning family. Whatever faults Shannon O'Rourke might have, holding a grudge didn't appear to be one of them.

"So, what did you want?" she asked.

Alex hesitated. He didn't *want* anything, but for Jeremy's sake he should keep things cordial between them. "It's just…I'm sorry I upset you. And I want you to know that I appreciated the way you handled Jeremy. That's all."

"Oh." Confusion filled her eyes.

A woman as beautiful as Shannon O'Rourke probably expected to be asked for a date, but he had no intention of getting involved with anyone, much less someone like Shannon. His friends and colleagues, everyone, kept saying it was just a matter of time, that if you've had one good marriage, you're more likely to have a second good one.

But he didn't buy it.

With Kim he'd gotten lucky, because he sure wasn't good husband material, not with his family background of domestic warfare and divorce. God, he'd hated all the screaming and fighting.

"Sir," called the postal clerk with an edge of irritation in her voice. "There are a lot of people waiting."

"Better go." Shannon flipped her hand and pushed through the double glass doors.

Alex released a harsh breath as he watched the gentle

sway of her hips as she headed for her car. Kim had been gone for almost a year. There wasn't any reason to feel guilty for enjoying a woman's legs.

Except he *did* feel guilty.

The rustle of restless feet and throat-clearing dragged his attention back to the post office. He returned to the counter and signed the credit slip, accompanied by applause from the line of postal customers. He walked outside with Jeremy while Shannon was still waiting to pull into the busy street, and his son dragged his feet, watching sadly as her sleek sports car finally merged into traffic.

"Come along, son."

"I like her, Daddy."

"I know. I'm sure you'll see her again. Shannon is our next-door neighbor."

Jeremy let out a very adult sigh. "But you made her mad."

It was undeniably true, even though she'd appeared to forgive what he'd jokingly implied about her brother. Yes, Shannon O'Rourke was temperamental, but she'd also shown that she was loyal.

A far cry from his own family.

After his parents divorced, Alex and his two siblings had been pawns in their incessant power struggles. And now they didn't see one another anymore. They were too far-flung for one thing; his brother was in the Arctic studying global warming and his sister was working in Japan. As for his mother and father, they'd each been married and divorced several times to other people, and they still hated each other with a passion that poisoned everything around them.

"Shannon isn't upset with you," he said finally. "So it's okay."

"But she's mad at you, Daddy." Jeremy was obstinate

in his own way, and he obviously felt that Shannon being mad was a problem, regardless of who she was mad at.

Alex rubbed the back of his neck. After his rotten up-bringing, he'd worried he couldn't love a child. But from the minute his newborn son, all red and wrinkled, opened sleepy eyes and blew a bubble at him, he'd turned into a marshmallow where the kid was concerned.

"I know, son, but you still don't need to worry about it." He would have said everything was "all right," but he'd said it too often when Kim was sick, and he'd felt like a hypocrite each time Jeremy crawled into his arms and believed him.

His son gave him an exasperated look, which would have been comical if his eyes weren't so serious. "Can we get her a Christmas present?"

A Christmas present?

What did you get for a woman who must have everything?

"We'll get a poinsettia," Alex promised. Plants were usually safe, especially since it should look like a seasonal gesture. Or as an apology for the verbal faux pas he'd stumbled into over her brother.

Jeremy looked relieved, and as they trudged back to the Cherokee, he turned his head to gaze in the direction Shannon had driven. For the first time in a year he wasn't clutch-ing Mr. Tibbles to his chest; instead, he was casually swinging the rabbit by one arm.

Alex let out a sigh of his own. He had to be careful. See-ing too much of the woman next door could lead Jeremy into getting ideas about a new mommy.

Yet as he fastened his son into the child's car seat, Alex couldn't help thinking about Shannon. She was undoubt-edly headstrong and opinionated, as different from his wife as a woman could be. He'd considered casual dating since

Kim's death, but none of the women he'd met were particularly interesting.

And none of them were like Shannon O'Rourke.

Chapter Two

Shannon let herself into the condo and tossed her purse onto the couch before plugging in the lights on the Christmas tree. She had to be out of her mind even to have *considered* offering to babysit.

"Me, babysitting. Hah!"

Yet even as she scolded herself, she remembered Jeremy McKenzie's solemn blue eyes and a familiar ache filled her. She'd been eight when her father died, leaving her confused and hurt. The thought of Jeremy feeling the same way tore at her heart.

"I'm not the motherly type," she muttered. She couldn't change a diaper or even heat a can of soup, though Jeremy was surely old enough not to need diapers any longer. Even that she wasn't certain about, though she was pretty sure most kids were potty-trained by the time they were two or three. How old were her twin nieces when they'd stopped needing diapers? It was embarrassing to realize she didn't know. They were her nieces, and she loved them dearly. Sinking into the chair next to the phone, Shannon dialed her youngest sister.

"Hey, Kathleen. When did Amy and Peggy get potty-trained?" she asked without preamble.

"Shannon?"

"Yes. How old were they?"

"Er…not quite two."

Two. Well, that was good. Undoubtedly kids developed differently, but Jeremy was probably past that stage. Not that it mattered. Alex McKenzie hadn't given any sign of being interested in her, so she wasn't likely to see much of either him or his son.

It was so depressing. Her love life was a disaster area. She wanted an honest relationship with the right man, but what if the "right" man didn't want someone like her?

"What's up, Shannon?"

She shrugged, though her sister couldn't see the gesture. "A little boy moved in next door, that's all. He's really cute, and I started thinking about diapers and stuff. It doesn't mean anything, except I got curious."

"Are you sure that's all?"

"Positive."

Shannon said good-bye and dropped the receiver with disgust. It had to be her biological clock ticking that made her ask stupid questions. She was twenty-eight years old and unmarried—and unlikely ever to be married at the rate she was going, so of course her clock was screaming.

Shaking her head, Shannon walked up to the bedroom to change into a pair of sweats and then began to run on the treadmill in her spare room.

She had a great family, a terrific job, made plenty of

money, and was perfectly comfortable, she told herself in time with her steps. It wasn't the end of the world if the love of her life never showed up. Of course, it was hard to keep believing that with the rest of the world obsessed with love, and her own family acting as if Cupid had gone target-happy with his bow and arrows. Even Neil, her brother who had once equated marriage with the plague, had fallen off the deep end. So now Neil had Libby. Her oldest brother, Kane, had Beth and baby daughter, Robin. Patrick had Maddie and their new son, Jarod. Dylan and his wife, Kate, were expecting a baby. Only her youngest brother, Connor, was still unattached. Of course, her sisters weren't married, though Kathleen was divorced. Shannon grimaced at the thought of Kathleen's ex-husband. There were worse things than being single…like having a cheating spouse who'd run off when you were almost nine months pregnant with twins.

A half hour later the doorbell rang and Shannon stopped the machine. She wiped her face with a towel, grabbed a bottle of water from the fridge and took a swig on her way to the door.

"Who is that?" she called on her way downstairs to the door.

She peeped through the curtain and gulped at the sight of Alex and Jeremy McKenzie.

"Isn't this just perfect?" she mumbled. Her face was flushed, her hair damp, and she was wearing an old pair of sweats. Well, it couldn't be helped, so she lifted her chin and squared her shoulders as she opened the door. You could get through the worst situation by acting as if you owned the world.

"Hi."

"Hello." Alex's velvet-rough voice rubbed over her edgy nerves like a silky cat. "Jeremy wanted to be sure you weren't mad at us."

Mad?

Shannon thought for a moment, then recalled the way Alex had seemed to mock Kane, her darling oldest brother. She was willing to give him a second chance, especially with Jeremy looking at her with that anxious expression in his eyes.

"I'm not mad," she said, looking down at Jeremy and smiling. He really was the dearest child, with such a sweet, sad, worried little face. No wonder her scant motherly instincts were clamoring for attention. How could anyone fail to adore him?

"It's for you," Jeremy said, holding out a poinsettia wrapped in green foil and banded by a big gold ribbon and bow. "Can we come in?"

"Of course you may," Shannon said over Alex's attempts to shush his son. She stepped back and raised an eyebrow.

"Thank you," Alex muttered.

"Ooooh," exclaimed Jeremy. He'd marched into the center of the living room, and stared transfixed at the Christmas tree, winking and glowing in the corner.

Alex understood his son's fascination. It was a great tree, and at its base a small train ran around and around a miniature Victorian town at the foot of a snowy mountain. The houses were lit, ice-skaters twirled around a silver lake, and even the small street lamps twinkled.

"Sorry about how I look, you caught me exercising," Shannon said. She made no attempt at feminine fussing, and since she was flat-out beautiful with her healthy flush and sexy, mussed hair, it wasn't necessary.

"You look fine," Alex muttered.

In the soft glow from the Christmas tree her hair was a deep rich auburn, and he had a crazy urge to run his fingers through the silken strands, to discover if it was as soft as it looked. It occurred to him that she might not be a natural redhead since there wasn't a freckle in sight on her peach complexion, but he shoved the thought away. Whether she was or wasn't didn't concern him. And he'd certainly never see the proof.

"Well…thanks for the plant," Shannon said. She put it by the fireplace, smiling at Jeremy as he tore his gaze away from the tree. "This is so pretty. Did you pick it out all by yourself?"

"Uh-huh," he said.

"That was nice of you. You got the best poinsettia I've ever seen."

Jeremy's smile was like sunshine, and Alex blinked. Where was his shy little boy? The grief-stricken, barely talking, rabbit-clutching four-year-old?

"Mr. Tibbles said to get that one."

"You and Mr. Tibbles have good taste." She glanced at Alex. "I don't keep many treats around the house, but are lemon drops on the okay list?"

"They're fine," he agreed, still bemused.

Shannon took a crystal dish from the mantel and removed the lid before offering its contents to Jeremy. Soon his son was sucking on lemon sours and playing with the controls of the train gliding around the extravagant Christmas tree. Steam even came from the top of the engine when a button was pressed on the control panel. Jeremy seemed to enjoy that part especially, along with the train's abrupt stops and starts.

Alex warned Jeremy to be careful, but Shannon seemed unconcerned that the expensive set might be in danger.

"It's all right," she said. "Would you like some soda?"

"We don't want to be any trouble."

"If you were trouble, I'd tell you."

Undoubtedly she would. Shannon O'Rourke was direct, self-assured and definitely wouldn't pussyfoot around. She was also the walking, talking embodiment of everything he'd avoided his entire life—an explosion of emotion and passion wrapped up in flame-colored hair and flashing eyes.

"Tell you what," she said. "If you haven't eaten dinner yet, we can order some pizza. I'm out of milk for Jeremy, but maybe they can bring some with the delivery."

He wanted to say no. He even opened his mouth to say no, only one look at his son's ecstatic face changed his mind. Jeremy loved pizza, but his mother had declared it was unhealthy for children, so they'd rarely eaten any. Come to think of it, he wasn't sure why Kim had disapproved of restaurant and take-out food so much, but she had.

"That sounds good," he agreed. "But it's my treat."

"Whatever. The phone's over there with the phone book, so go ahead and order. I'm going upstairs to change."

"Any preferences?"

"No anchovies, that's all." She glanced at Jeremy. He looked hopeful, and she tried to guess what he might be wishing his daddy would order. "How about one of those dessert pizzas, too? One with lots of sugar and stuff on top." Jeremy's face turned blissful and she winked at him.

Shannon climbed the staircase to her bedroom and willed her heart to stop beating so fast. She'd figured the post office was the last close contact she'd get with Alex

McKenzie and his son, but now they were in her living room and her pulse was doing the Macarena.

She took a quick shower, then pulled on a pair of jeans and a sweater. Her footsteps were muffled on the thickly carpeted stairs, so when she descended to the living room, she was able to observe Alex and his son without them being aware of her presence.

With a quiet sigh she sat on a step and watched.

The two of them were lying on their stomachs, side by side, gazing at the tree and the train set her decorator sister, Miranda, had arranged for her a few days after Thanksgiving. This year, Miranda had outdone herself, creating a Victorian holiday wonderland out of the living room.

"Choo, choo!" crowed Jeremy as the train chugged through the tunnel in the snowcapped mountain.

He was darling, yet it was Alex who drew her gaze the longest, his jeans pulled taut over long, strong legs and a tight rear end. He didn't look like any college professor she'd ever studied with, or else she would have paid more attention in class. His rugged good looks had probably turned engineering into a very popular subject—with the female students, at least.

Shannon's eyes drifted half-closed as she imagined what it would be like to be married to someone like Alex.

It was a great fantasy, but reality kept intruding. Alex had said his wife had loved baking and doing crafts and making Christmas special; he'd probably be shocked that she had her home professionally decorated every year and couldn't bake a cookie to save her life. Even Shannon's mother had declared defeat in teaching her eldest daughter how to cook.

The doorbell rang and she jumped up.

"That must be our pizza," she said brightly.

They ate in front of the tree, sitting cross-legged and using the napkins provided by the delivery guy.

"Mommy didn't let us eat pizza," Jeremy said after a while, then looked even more worried than before.

"She didn't?" It seemed odd, but there might have been reasons Shannon knew nothing about, like allergies or another problem.

"Uh-uh." He glanced quickly at his father, then carefully put his crust down on a napkin. "I get afraid, 'cause I don't r'member her so good anymore."

Alex looked pained, and Shannon bit the inside of her lip. Jeremy had been so young when his mother died, it was inevitable his memories were fading.

She put her forefinger over Jeremy's heart, the way her own mother used to do when her youngest sister had worried about forgetting their father.

"You'll always remember her in here," she said softly. "That's the most important kind of remembering. Your mommy is always right here, so you don't need to be afraid."

The youngster seemed to think about it, then nodded, looking more cheerful. His father handed him a piece of dessert pizza and they ate in silence until Jeremy looked up, his expression brightening.

"Daddy, I bet if Shannon was my new mommy, we could eat pizza whenever we wanted."

Shannon inhaled a crumb and choked. Between coughing, thumps on the back from Alex and her eyes tearing, the moment passed without either of them having to say anything.

Cripes.

How did you handle a remark like that?

"I think it's time for us to go home," Alex said when her windpipe had finally cleared. His face had become closed. "We've imposed long enough on Miss O'Rourke."

"But, Daddy, we—"

"It's time to go, son."

Jeremy's mouth turned down mutinously, but he didn't object again. Shannon insisted they take the last of the pizza, and she sank against the door as she closed it behind them, exhausted.

She didn't know what the expression on Alex's face had meant, but he obviously did not share his son's enthusiasm for getting a new mommy. He didn't know her well enough to object to her personally, so it must be the idea of marrying again that had him feeling grief or guilt or another of the thousand emotions a widower must feel.

Not that it mattered. She just wanted to help Jeremy. Right?

But as Shannon gathered up the crumpled napkins and put the dirty glasses in the sink, she couldn't shake the melancholy that had overtaken her. It was painfully obvious she was attracted to old-fashioned men, no matter what she'd told herself about wanting a modern guy with modern attitudes. And Alex McKenzie made her nerve endings stand at attention more than any man she'd met in recent memory.

It doesn't matter one way or the other, she told herself. Men usually were drawn to the same kind of woman, and from the little she'd learned about Alex's dead wife, she wasn't the least bit like her.

"I'm going back to work," Shannon told Kane a few days later. Her brother and his wife, Beth, had come to their mother's house for a visit and she'd joined them, more on edge than ever. Not that seeing her brother had helped. Kane's blissfully happy marriage was another reminder of how alone she felt.

"I don't think so."

"Kane, I want—"

"You've been stressed out, you need to relax," Kane interrupted. He finished diapering his daughter and lifted the baby to his shoulder. Robin looked even tinier against his broad chest, and something inside Shannon ached with renewed force. It was yet another reminder of everything she wanted, and couldn't seem to get.

"I'm fine."

"You can't spend your entire life working," Kane pointed out. His advice would have sounded reasonable except that before he'd gotten married he used to work more hours than she'd ever thought of putting into the company.

Shannon's mother patted her arm. "That's right, darlin'." Her Irish accent lilted, never quite lost despite the years she'd spent away from her native land.

"I'm fine. It's being on a forced vacation that's driving me crazy."

That, and thinking about the McKenzies.

She'd realized that Alex's bedroom was on the other side of the wall from hers, and that knowledge was keeping her awake nights. The walls were too well insulated to hear his bed creak, but she heard other faint sounds and couldn't help wondering about certain things.

Innocent things.

Such as...did he sleep nude at night?

Yeah, that was innocent.

Perfectly innocent.

It had been awhile since she'd thought about a man that way. Her last relationship had turned into such a disaster that she'd become frozen. Now she was thawing, and it was just her luck that a guaranteed heartbreak was the reason.

"You're still on vacation," Kane said calmly. He rubbed the baby's back and smiled at Shannon's frustrated expression.

"You can't be so arbitrary just because I'm your sister."

"I'd do the same for any executive with signs of burnout. You're still getting paid, so what's the big deal?"

"I am not burned-out."

"Then what's wrong?"

Shannon swallowed.

After their father had died, she'd decided she would be the tough one, the one who teased and laughed and smiled when she didn't feel like smiling. If she had trouble at school, she braved things out. If her heart got broken, she turned it into a joke—just so long as nobody found her crying in bed and upsetting her family. Over the years she'd perfected a breezy veneer that made everyone think she was impervious to the usual hurts and disappointments. She was an expert on putting on a good face; now was the time to prove it.

"Nothing is wrong," Shannon said, waving her hand. "It's the holiday season and people slack off. I must have gone overboard trying to keep my staff geared up for any problems that might happen."

Kane nodded, his gaze searching her face. He didn't seem entirely convinced, though he appeared less concerned than before. "All right. But I promised everyone they'd have another few days without the dragon lady, so you'll have to stay away longer."

She wrinkled her nose, making certain none of her frustration showed. "Dragon lady? Thanks a bunch. Is it too late for me to cancel a few Christmas bonuses?"

He chuckled. "Way too late."

Shannon kept things light through lunch, working to get her mother, brother and sister-in-law laughing. But it was a relief when she pulled out of her mother's driveway, escaping their watchful gazes. She drove for a long time, up into the hills, finally swinging by Neil's house.

She frowned as she tapped her fingers on the steering wheel and gazed at the modern log structure. She would have sworn that Neil, of all her brothers, would never get married and live outside the city, but he'd fallen for Libby like a ton of bricks. *Two* tons.

Sighing, Shannon headed home, deciding not to call Neil and his wife.

A winter sunset burned pink and gold on the western horizon as she finally pulled into her driveway, but she didn't have time to appreciate it before Jeremy flew across the yard, waving madly with one arm, the other clutching Mr. Tibbles.

An involuntary smile curved her mouth.

"Hey, Jeremy," she said, opening the car door.

"Hey, Shannon."

They had exchanged a few hellos and good-byes over the past few days, with Alex then hustling his son away with insulting speed. Of course, the speed might have been due to Washington's beastly winter weather, but it was still a little insulting.

"What have you been up to?" she asked as she got out.

"Daddy 'n' me are putting up Christmas lights," Jeremy said solemnly.

She noticed an expandable ladder leaning against the McKenzies' condo. "That's nice."

"But he got hurted and said a bad word."

Alex had followed his son across the yard, and Shannon glanced at him, trying not to laugh at his chagrined expression. She guessed his injury was relatively minor since there wasn't any visible blood and no bones were sticking out.

"He did?"

"Uh-huh. He said—"

"Jeremy," Alex interrupted hastily, "I was wrong to say that in the first place, and it certainly isn't something to repeat in front of a lady."

The youngster quieted and clutched Mr. Tibbles even tighter, mumbling an apology, so Shannon smiled and ruffled his hair.

"That's okay. I'm lucky, I have five brothers to help put up my Christmas lights." Five brothers with the same sort of old-fashioned views about a "lady's" delicate ears and sensibilities—all part of the O'Rourke Code they'd been taught by their father. The "Code" was sacred to the male members of the family, much to the frequent frustration of the *female* members.

"I wish I had a brother," Jeremy said, sounding wistful.

Oh dear.

Wasn't wishing he had a brother just one step away from talking about getting a new mommy? Presuming he understood the relationship between the two events.

"I also have three sisters," Shannon said quickly. "Miranda, Kelly and Kathleen. Miranda and Kelly are twins."

"Do they like dodgeball?"

Dodgeball? She searched through her memory and

vaguely recalled kids standing in a circle, with others in the middle dodging a large red ball.

"Uh, they haven't played for a while. They're all grown up."

Jeremy sighed. "I wanna play dodgeball, but the big kids say I'm too small."

"That's too bad, but they probably want to be sure you don't get hurt accidentally."

Alex stuck his throbbing thumb in his pocket and watched Shannon O'Rourke charm his son all over again. Jeremy's gaze was fixed on her adoringly, and he was talking like a normal little boy, rather than a traumatized child.

He'd asked around and learned a great deal about the O'Rourkes since meeting Shannon. People in all walks of life counted them as friends. They were highly respected, were active in church and charity work, and gave generously of both their time and their money. Shannon served on the boards of three foundations and was personally credited with saving an inner-city homeless mission.

No wonder, he thought, staring at her stunning beauty and trademark smile—a smile that said she was ready to take on the world single-handedly. The force of her personality alone was probably enough to save a hundred homeless missions, much less one. She was so…electric.

He smothered a half laugh, remembering the way people had described Shannon as cool and sophisticated. They were blind if they couldn't see the wildfire beneath that polished surface.

"Hello, Shannon," he murmured, illogically annoyed that she'd barely noticed him. Once upon a time the opposite sex had found him reasonably attractive.

Yet even as Alex formed the thought, he stomped on it.

Shannon O'Rourke might be a beautiful woman, but he'd rather appreciate her beauty from a distance. He didn't have to own Botticelli's *Birth of Venus* to admire the painting.

"Hello." Shannon smiled. "Are you having trouble putting up your Christmas lights?"

"Some." Alex flexed his thumb and a sharp throb went through it. He'd been distracted, thinking about Jeremy and the day-care center's third request for the name and phone number of a backup person to call in case of emergency. He had a babysitter for when the daycare was closed, but except for Shannon, there wasn't a single person in Washington with whom Jeremy would willingly go if his father wasn't available. That was the problem. Shannon was good with Jeremy and had an excellent reputation so there wasn't any reason not to ask…besides wanting to keep that precious distance between them.

Damn.

Around Shannon he felt as if he was being sucked into a whirlpool with no bottom. The sensation reminded him too much of when he was a kid and had no control over his life, or the crazy people masquerading as his parents.

"If you're hungry, I was going to order some Thai food for dinner," she said, breaking into his thoughts. "You're welcome to join me."

He hesitated.

"Consider it a welcome to the neighborhood," she said breezily. "I should have brought you cookies or something, but…" Her voice trailed and she shrugged.

That *but* had some interesting undertones to it. Shannon had a way of saying things that had so many layers of meaning, he could get dizzy trying to figure them out.

"Yeah, you blew your chance of being nominated for the

neighborhood welcome party," he said, trying to sound humorous. "Tami Barton made us a casserole. Naomi Hale did Jell-O salad, and Lisa Steeple brought us a cake. And there's also been homemade candy, cookies, several kinds of bread and some sort of cheese log rolled in almonds."

"Let me guess, mostly from the unmarried women in the condo association? I know Naomi, Tami, and Lisa are all unattached."

Alex frowned, realizing there *had* been quite a few single women—divorced or never married—knocking on his door lately. It had been the same in Minnesota. After Kim's death few days had gone by without a knock on the door and a woman standing on the other side. Their culinary offerings had ranged from child-pleasing dishes to gourmet meals. It was one of the reasons he'd come to Seattle, trying to get away from would-be mothers, looking for a ready-made family. Hell. He must have been blind not to see the pattern. Lisa and Naomi had been too friendly, but he'd ignored their flirting the way he'd always ignored feminine overtures that didn't come from his wife.

A pang went through him as he reminded himself that Kim was gone. He'd never put much thought into the marriage vow "till death do us part." Women usually lived longer than men, and he'd figured he'd go first. But he hadn't gone first, and now he had to deal with a reality that didn't include Kim.

His stomach turned as emotions crawled through it, a reminder of those horrible, empty days after the funeral, when he'd cursed himself and God…and his wife for being human enough to get leukemia and die.

"Alex?"

"Yeah," he said tightly. "They were mostly single."

Shannon's gaze flicked over him, seeming almost as tangible as a touch. "I may be single, but I promise not to bake you any cakes or cookies."

"Skip the Jell-O salad and casseroles, too, okay?" Alex muttered. He didn't want anything that reminded him of the food at Kim's wake.

"I promise." Once again something unknown flickered in Shannon's expressive face, but he couldn't begin to guess at the meaning. "And you can skip the offer of Thai food, if you prefer. I may be single, but I'm not on the prowl like Lisa or the others."

"What's 'on the prowl'?" Jeremy asked.

He was examining them both with his serious eyes, and Alex saw that Shannon was as nonplussed as he was over the question. For some reason it reassured him. She was so darned confident about everything, it was nice to know there were some things she wasn't certain how to handle.

"It means that Shannon just wants to be our friend," Alex said.

"That's right," she added quickly. "Just friends."

The emphasis she put on the words drained some of the satisfaction from Alex, which just proved how illogical he could be. The last thing he needed was a neighbor who saw him a potential mate, particularly a neighbor as unsettling as Shannon.

Chapter Three

"Actually, Thai sounds good," Alex found himself saying to his astonishment. "But Jeremy may not like something so different."

"That's all right. I can ask the delivery guy to pick up a hamburger on the way over. Does that sound good to you, Jeremy? We'll have him get french fries, too."

Naturally, Jeremy looked thrilled. He loved fast food, particularly since his mother hadn't allowed him to eat any. Alex had tried to stick to Kim's rules about their son's diet, but convenience foods were called convenient for a reason...they were convenient.

It wasn't that he couldn't cook. His work had taken him to some remote parts of the world where restaurants didn't exist. You learned to cook or you didn't eat. But between work and trying to spend time with Jeremy, it was easier to grab a bag of precut salad mix and a microwave dinner. Now that things were becoming more settled, they would have to start a routine that made them both comfortable.

"That would be fine," Alex said. "Except I doubt you can get the delivery person to run an errand for you."

Shannon's smile turned even more beguiling. "Wanna bet?"

No.

He definitely didn't want to bet.

She could probably charm a perfect stranger into doing something they had no intention of doing. Like him, for example. He'd fully intended to keep his distance, and now they were having dinner together again. He had to be out of his mind.

"You can try the Thai food if you want," Shannon told Jeremy as they went up her walkway. "I just love the peanut chicken. It's sweet and yummy."

"Uh…okay."

They chattered away and Alex nodded in resignation as his son agreed to try a few of the exotic dishes Shannon enthused about. One of the few discordant notes in his marriage had been Kim's lack of culinary adventure, and Jeremy was just as stubborn about trying new things…or had been until now. His son had done nothing but talk about Shannon ever since meeting her, so he'd probably eat live worms if she asked.

"Any preferences?" Shannon asked Alex as she hung her coat in the entry closet. Unlike her orderly living room, the closet was an untidy mess of winter gear and sports equipment. He supposed it was a sort of metaphor, representing the variable sides of her nature. "I like almost everything, so speak up for whatever you want."

Spicy, he wanted to say, but was afraid it would come

out sounding seductive. Curiously, her sexual impact was both subtle and overt. The overt part didn't bother him. It was the subtle, vulnerable part of her that had him ready to bark at the moon.

Yet even as the thought formed, Alex shook his head in denial. He doubted there was a vulnerable cell in Shannon O'Rourke's delectable body. She was bright and fiery, like the shining surface of a diamond. Sure, she had a soft spot for his son and seemed to care about people who were less fortunate, but vulnerable?

Not a chance.

"I've learned to like most everything, too, with all the traveling I've done," he said. "But if you hope Jeremy will try something new, I'd get mild." He nearly added *and don't get your hopes up,* then decided Shannon would find out soon enough about his son's preference for unimaginative food.

She picked up the phone. "That's fine. I'll ask them to put some crushed red pepper on the side."

In a short time she'd ordered a number of dishes and sweet-talked the manager into having the delivery driver pick up a burger, fries and a carton of milk.

"I think you ordered too much," Alex said.

"Not if you have a big appetite like my brothers."

Shannon's comfortable references to her family made Alex uneasily aware that he rarely spoke to his own relatives, even during the holidays.

"You're close to them, aren't you?" he asked curiously.

"Of course I am. Naturally they drive me crazy trying to interfere with my life. And Kane takes his position as head of the family way too seriously, but they aren't bad for big lugs with the mentality of cavemen."

His eyebrows shot upward. "Cavemen?"

"Completely. You should have seen the way they acted when I started dating."

Alex smiled. "That bad, eh?"

"Worse. I swear that Kane or Neil or Patrick followed me on every date for the first six months. Even Dylan and Connor were weird about it. Do you know what it's like to be unable to enjoy your first kiss for fear one of your brothers is going to pounce?"

"Not really." Alex choked, fighting a laugh.

Shannon was trying to sound aggrieved, but he could tell she was touched by her brothers' protectiveness. Yet he sobered quickly, wondering if his own sister had ever had trouble when she started dating, and if she'd ever wished her brothers were there to protect her.

He'd been long gone to college and building his career by the time Gail was old enough to start going out with boys.

"Did you ever have trouble on a date? One you needed help handling?" he murmured.

"Me? Not a chance. I take care of myself."

Something flashed through Shannon's eyes so quickly, it was gone almost before it registered.

She was lying.

Not in a bad way. Just covering up something she didn't like remembering, or didn't want to confess.

It bothered him that Shannon might not be as tough as she appeared—maybe because her brothers were still protecting her, while he'd seen Gail just once in the past three years. Gail was tough, too; you didn't grow up in the McKenzie household without developing a protective shell. But what if his sister wasn't as tough as he thought?

Because it raised a confusing array of emotions that

Alex didn't want to feel, he sat next to Jeremy, who was playing once again with Shannon's Christmas train set.

"Choo, choo," Jeremy chanted. Mr. Tibbles had been leaned up against one of the miniature Victorian houses, and he looked decidedly tipsy with one of his long ears flopped over a black button eye.

Sometimes Alex hated that rabbit.

It represented the dark days, the loss his little boy never should have suffered. Only the introduction of Shannon into their lives had lessened his fierce attachment to Mr. Tibbles.

Shannon...

Sighing to himself, Alex glanced across the room. She'd knelt by the fireplace and was lighting a neatly laid stack of logs. The sway of her hips beneath her formfitting jeans made him uncomfortably warm. Her impact on his senses was the most likely explanation for his agreeing to dinner, but knowing that didn't make him happy.

He cleared his throat. "I'm surprised you don't have a gas fire. It's more convenient."

She turned and smiled. "I prefer the light and warmth of a real fire."

"Gas puts off heat and light."

"Not like this." Shannon gazed into the new flames licking across the wood, a dreamy expression on her face. "Every year I visit Ireland with my mother. The cottage she grew up in has a fireplace that fills most of a wall in the kitchen. The light bounces off the polished copper pots and kettles, and it feels so safe and secure, as if nothing will ever change."

"Everything changes." The words came out sharper than Alex had intended, but it was the truth. Things changed, no matter how much he disliked the process.

The corners of Shannon's mouth turned down, and the soft light of memory faded from her eyes. "I know. That's a lesson I received when I wasn't many years older than Jeremy. Anyway, my grandparents still live in the cottage, though Kane wants to build them a modern house with modern conveniences, either in Ireland or here in Washington."

Alex found himself moving closer, drawn partly by the warmth in his lower extremities, and partly by the unguarded emotions he'd seen in her face. "They refused?"

"Yes. Generations of Scanlons have grown up there, and they're not ones to be goin' anywhere that God didn't put them." She said the last in a distinct brogue, and he knew she was repeating something she must have heard often from her faraway grandparents.

"I take it your grandparents didn't approve of your mother going to America."

"It was my father they didn't approve of. That is…" Her voice trailed, and to Alex's surprise, Shannon looked shy, as if she'd revealed something she thought should have stayed private. "They're good people, but my father was wild before he married my mother, and then he took her thousands of miles away."

Wild?

"You take after your father, don't you?" he asked before he could think better of the question. He didn't need to know those kinds of things about Shannon; they weren't even friends, much less lovers.

"Yes, though my third-oldest brother is the most like Dad. Of course, Patrick is settling down now, too. He got married a couple of months after Kane."

"Is marriage the answer for your family? Like a ship's anchor for all that wildness?"

"Maybe." Shannon flipped a curling lock of auburn hair away from her face, and shrugged. "But probably not for me."

Once again there was a confusing emotion in her green eyes, quickly concealed. A man could get whiplash trying to figure her out, and for the hundredth time Alex's head warned him to get out, now, before he got involved. Women like Shannon might be fascinating, but they were also too disturbing.

Despite the warning, he leaned forward. "Why not you?"

"Lots of reasons," she said lightly. "I'm too independent and want things my own way. I enjoy working and keeping my own hours, that sort of stuff."

Once again he had the oddest sensation, as though she'd told him something that wasn't entirely true.

"Seeing how good you are with kids, I'd think you'd want a family of your own."

She lifted an eyebrow. "How do you know I'm good with kids? Maybe it's just a fluke with Jeremy."

Alex laughed. "I don't believe that. Why else would he respond to you?"

"It's…complicated." Shannon's smile trembled and she looked at Jeremy playing with the train set. Her voice lowered. "I think it's because I understand what he's going through. You see, my father died in an accident when I was eight. One minute I was a happy, carefree little girl, and the next…"

Her eyes blinked rapidly, unnaturally bright, and he winced. "Don't, Shannon."

She shook her head. "No, I want you to understand, because if there's anything I can do to help Jeremy, I want to do it. I know how it feels to be young and have your world fall apart, and to hurt so much you want to crawl in a hole and hide," she said, sounding as if the words had been dragged from a deep place in her soul, a place she didn't usually reveal.

Alex felt like a heel for causing her to speak about something so painful. Maybe it wasn't such a terrible thing to ask for her phone number to give the day-care center. Jeremy came first, and Shannon obviously wanted to help.

He raked a hand through his hair, his need to stay uninvolved battling with the seductive desire to be close to a woman as tempting as Shannon. And right in the middle of the battle were his son's needs, more important than anything else.

"Actually, there is something…well, there's a favor you could do for us," he said slowly.

Shannon raised one eyebrow when he fell silent. "Yes?" she prompted.

"The day-care center has been asking for an emergency contact in case they can't reach me. I know it's a lot to ask, but they're right about needing someone local. I understand if you don't want to. It's really all right if you say no."

Alex sent up a prayer she would say no, or seem reluctant, or say something else that would get him off the hook. Then he could honestly stall the day-care center again.

"Of course," Shannon said, reaching for her purse and taking out a business card. She scribbled something on the back and handed it to him. "This has my office number, and I put down my home and cell, along with my executive assistant's phone. She can always reach me. Really, if there's anything you need, just call."

God in heaven…

She was so generous, and Alex gazed into her green eyes for an endless moment, then down at the curves of her mouth. Panic lapped at the edge of his consciousness; he didn't want to be attracted to Shannon or be pulled into her world. He wanted things to be calm and sane, with everything in its proper place. He needed things to be that way.

The doorbell rang before Alex could sort through the emotional minefield he'd stumbled into, and he let out an unconscious sigh of relief. "That must be dinner."

He pulled out his wallet, but Shannon shook her head. "It's my treat, remember?"

Letting a woman pay for dinner went against the grain. "But—"

"No 'buts.'" Shannon got to her feet. It had been years since she'd had so much trouble keeping herself from blushing, yet something about Alex was making her say things she never planned on saying.

And those eyes of his...they were too darned intent. She'd bet anything that he wasn't thinking about her the way she kept thinking about him, but that was the story of her love life. Men always had a different agenda, and how was she supposed to figure out a man who'd lost his wife and was worried about his son?

"So, how is everything going with your classes?" she asked after they'd settled at the dining-room table and spooned various portions onto their plates, the food steaming and spicing the air with the pungent fragrances of lemongrass and other herbs.

Alex groaned. "Okay, but I didn't have any idea how tough it was teaching basic engineering principles to undergrads."

"I thought you'd been teaching for a long time."

"No, this is my first year. I used to work on engineering projects all over the world. But now that it's just me and Jeremy, I realized that moving every few months for a job wasn't the right life for him."

"It must have been easier to manage a nomadic life-style with three of you."

He glanced at Jeremy and looked uncomfortable. "It wasn't like that. I enjoy spending time in remote, primitive locations, but Kim didn't feel that way, so she stayed in our house back in Minnesota. I'd fly home as often as possible, but she wanted to have a stable base, especially after Jeremy came. It was for the best."

The best for who?

It wasn't Shannon's business, but it sounded awful. Families belonged together. Her mother had picked up the family and moved with Keenan O'Rourke whenever necessary. They'd lived all over the Seattle region when Shannon was a kid, though mostly in small towns, rather than the city.

"Maybe you should consider working with graduate students," she murmured instead of speaking her mind the way she wanted. Alex's wife had made her decisions; there wasn't any point in criticizing them. "You might enjoy it more."

"They're assigning me a group of graduates after the first of the year. And I guess it isn't that bad," he said thoughtfully. "I miss the work more than the travel, but it's an interesting challenge to mold future engineers."

"How about doing consulting on the side?"

"I've thought about that, but it's taken longer than I expected to get settled."

Shannon made a mental note to talk to Kane. Her

brother hired the brightest and best for his company, and she didn't doubt that Alex McKenzie fell into that category. Of course, if she said anything to Kane about Alex, he'd ask questions she didn't want to answer.

Jeremy sat watching them and she noticed a frown growing on his small face. She hadn't said anything more about him eating some of the Thai food, not wanting him to dig his heels in and refuse. She'd simply put the hamburger and fries in front of him, and waited.

"You said I could try some," he announced abruptly.

"That's right. What do you want to try first?"

He pointed to her plate.

"Mmm, yummy choice. That's the peanut chicken I told you about. It's sweet, with ground peanuts and coconut milk." Shannon served some onto his plate, holding back on the fresh spinach that came with the chicken—there was no sense in pushing her luck. "There you go."

Jeremy regarded the food with the expression of a mouse confronting a lion, but he slowly picked up a fork. His smile brightened as he chewed, then quickly finished the sample she'd given him. "Can I have some more?"

On the other side of the table Alex stared in wonder. "*May* I have some more," he automatically corrected.

"Okay. Can Daddy have more, too?" Jeremy asked.

Shannon choked and Alex spotted the smile she was trying to hide. "Yes," she said, "your daddy may have more, too. You both can have anything you want."

Alex doubted that.

What he wanted, and what he should have, were two entirely different things. His attraction to Shannon was inappropriate, ill-timed and utterly impossible. For Jeremy's sake, as well as his own, he had to keep it hidden.

Just then she flicked a small amount of sauce from her lip with her tongue and his body hardened.

Keeping his response to Shannon hidden might not be easy, he thought with resignation.

Much later, after tucking Jeremy into bed, Alex stared into his own dark fireplace and brooded.

He liked sex.

Always had.

After getting married, he'd had opportunities to go to bed with other women, but the idea of being unfaithful to his wife was repugnant. Lack of fidelity, among other things, had cursed his parents' relationship.

What would Kim say if she knew he was having sensual thoughts about Shannon O'Rourke? He shook his head at the question. Kim would probably say something reasonable and measured like…those feelings are normal…don't beat yourself up over it…it's all right. Her Zenlike calm had irritated him sometimes, but he reminded himself it was what he'd wanted. His wife had rarely raised her voice, much less become angry.

He was back to square one, not knowing what to do about Shannon. She might be able to help Jeremy, but what if his son got more ideas about her becoming his new mommy?

And what if he got more ideas about taking her to bed?

Alex couldn't have a no-strings affair with his next-door neighbor. Besides, for all of Shannon's modern sophistication, he didn't think she was a "no-strings" type of woman.

He rubbed the back of his neck, trying to ease his tight muscles, but it was useless.

When had life gotten so damned complicated?

Chapter Four

Shannon sipped her cup of tea and glanced around the crowded coffee shop.

The Seattle area was a coffee lover's mecca, and cheerful Christmas shoppers filled the store to capacity. Couples seemed to be in force today, replete with loving looks and affectionate gestures toward one another. For some inexplicable reason the scene made her think about Alex McKenzie. On the other hand, maybe it wasn't inexplicable. *Everything* made her think about Alex.

Sighing, Shannon put her cup on a collection tray and slipped from the store.

Small leaves, scattered by a cold breeze, danced across the sidewalk and into the street. Another sigh escaped as her cell phone rang.

"Hello," she answered.

"Shannon, it's Alex."

She stopped dead in her tracks. "Alex. Hello."

"Are you in the middle of something?" His voice sounded oddly stressed and she frowned.

"I was doing some Christmas shopping, but I'm done now. Is something wrong?"

"No. That is, nothing serious. But I'm involved in something urgent, and Jeremy is at the day-care center. He says he isn't feeling well. I doubt it's anything, and I hate to ask, but I'm really—"

"I'd be happy to pick him up," Shannon said instantly. "He can stay with me until you get home." There was a long silence and she bit her lip. "Alex, are you there?"

"Yes. I appreciate the offer. I shouldn't be too late, I hope no later than mid afternoon." He gave her directions to the day-care center, then rang off.

Shannon stood stock-still for a minute, filled with both shock and alarm. She knew even less about sick children than she did about children in general.

"This isn't about you," she muttered, annoyed with herself. "It's about Jeremy."

It was also about Alex, and the confusing way he seemed to blow hot and cold. She'd hoped they could be friends after their second dinner together, but he'd sounded so uneasy telling her about Jeremy.

She shook her head.

Men were stubborn about asking for help. It seemed to wound their pride to think they couldn't handle everything themselves. Or maybe Alex's problem was something else— something even more incomprehensible than the male ego.

"And men claim women are unpredictable," Shannon muttered as she unlocked her car and jumped behind the wheel. Handling a sick little boy would probably be a piece of cake compared to dealing with a grown-up Alex.

At the day-care center an older woman met Shannon at the door. "Miss O'Rourke? Hello, I'm Helen Davis. Please come inside. I'm afraid Jeremy is upset."

"What happened?"

"We told him you were coming and he seemed pleased. Then one of our aides offered to mend his stuffed rabbit while he waited, and things went down from there."

Shannon's eyebrows shot upward. "She didn't try to take Mr. Tibbles away from Jeremy, did she?"

"Not…exactly."

"Shannon," yelped a small voice, and Jeremy raced forward, practically leaping into her arms. He clutched her neck with surprising strength.

"Hey, kiddo. It's okay."

He looked at her, his blue eyes brimming with tears. "The lady wanted to poke Mr. Tibbles with a needle." He scowled at Mrs. Davis as if she'd sprouted horns and a tail.

"That's too bad. Do you want to come home with me?"

"Uh-huh. Mr. Tibbles wants a nap."

Poor little guy. He couldn't admit he wanted to sleep, so Mr. Tibbles was taking the blame. Shannon stroked the dark hair away from Jeremy's forehead. He felt warm, but kids always felt warm to her.

"Let's go," she said quietly, carrying him out to the car.

When they arrived home, Shannon settled Jeremy in the living room. He quickly curled up on the floor with a pillow and blanket, Mr. Tibbles clutched to his chest. Sucking his thumb, he watched the cheerful village beneath the Christmas tree until he fell asleep.

Alex raced down the freeway, pushing the speed limit, a thousand things on his mind, including the frightened student he'd just left at the University Health Center.

Rita Sawyer, a brilliant sixteen-year-old prodigy, had come to him with a problem.

A *big* problem.

Big enough to make him call Shannon and ask for a favor he would have given almost anything not to ask.

Alex flexed his hands on the steering wheel, angry all over again. If he ever found out which football player had thought it was fun to seduce an underage girl, the slithering little snake would stop laughing in a hurry. Unfortunately, Rita had been too upset and scared to tell him who was responsible.

He pulled into the drive and regarded the side by side condos. Shannon's side glowed with warmth and welcome in the early twilight of the Washington winter day. His house seemed cold and aloof.

"Stop that," Alex ordered beneath his breath.

He wasn't a fanciful person. Buildings weren't endowed with anything more than brick and wood and plaster.

Shannon opened the door before he could knock and she put her finger to her lips. "Jeremy's asleep," she said softly. "I think he has a slight fever, but it doesn't seem bad."

"You mean he's really sick?"

He practically pushed Shannon to one side. It was only when he saw his son sleeping on a large pillow that his breathing slowed. One of Jeremy's arms was around Mr. Tibbles, and the other was stretched out to touch the controls of the toy train.

"God," Alex muttered, rubbing the back of his neck in an attempt to ease tense muscles. "He's been complaining of tummy aches and stuff every few days, asking to go home. The day-care center thought he was just crying wolf again."

Shannon sat next to Jeremy and stroked the hair from his forehead. It was such a naturally caring gesture that Alex's chest tightened. She seemed able to reach Jeremy when everyone else had failed. He didn't understand why—she was so different from Jeremy's mother.

"He might be getting a cold," she said softly. "But I doubt it's serious." Her auburn hair fell over her shoulders, spilling across a fuzzy white sweater. She looked like an angel, and Alex forced himself to look away, fixing his gaze on Jeremy.

There was nothing angelic about Shannon O'Rourke. Angels did not twist a man's guts into knots.

Seeming unaware of his scrutiny, she smiled and rose. "Would you like some soda, or maybe some wine? You look like you could use a drink."

"Cola, if you have it."

"I'll be back in a moment."

She disappeared into the kitchen and he heard the clinking of ice against glass. Still concerned, he knelt and felt his son's forehead for himself. Warmer than normal, but nothing serious.

Slumping down on the couch, Alex rubbed his face and tried to release the tension gripping him. Everything was all right. In a few days Jeremy probably wouldn't even remember it was Shannon who'd come to the rescue instead of his daddy.

Kids were resilient.

How many times had he heard that?

Doctors, child psychologists, pastors, well-meaning acquaintances—people felt they had to say something when they learned about Kim's death. Everyone had a support group they thought he should join, or a counselor to see...or a single female relative he should call, who was reputed to be a good listener.

He didn't need a good listener; he just needed to take care of his son and make sure nothing ever hurt Jeremy again.

Alex swallowed.

It was hard to escape the feeling that if he'd been home in Minnesota more often, Kim might have been diagnosed earlier. Another few weeks of treatment might have made the difference in her recovery. But he hadn't been there, and all the guilt in the world wouldn't change things now.

"Alex?" Shannon had emerged from the kitchen and was holding out a glass. He didn't know how long she'd waited to catch his attention, but a faint frown creased her forehead.

"Thanks. I appreciate you picking Jeremy up."

She shrugged one shoulder. "I told you I'd be happy to help out."

She astonished him. His parents had shown him that most people needed or wanted *something;* they didn't offer to help someone out of the goodness of their hearts. And a woman like Shannon, whom every wealthy bachelor in Washington must be chasing, certainly couldn't *need* or *want* a widower with a young son who wouldn't let go of his toy rabbit.

Alex cleared his throat. He could go nuts trying to figure out Shannon and her motives; she was far too complicated.

He accepted the glass, took a sip of the cola, then put the drink down on a polished wood coaster. It would be best if he made an excuse, took his son and left as soon as possible.

"So you think Jeremy has been trying to get attention by pretending to be sick?" she asked in a low tone.

"Yeah." Alex grabbed the cola again. "At least I did, but

now I don't know what to believe. If he's really ill…it's enough to make me crazy. I can't lose him."

"You aren't going to lose him," Shannon said softly. "Children get colds and tummy aches. It's rarely serious." She'd called her mom an hour earlier and been assured of that fact. "And children make up stories to get attention. It's part of being a kid."

Alex cocked his head. Weary lines bracketed his mouth and she wished she could smooth them away.

"Do you speak from experience?"

"Of course." She smiled. "My youngest sister put on 'dying diva' performances worthy of an Oscar. Fortunately my mother was less gullible than the rest of us."

"What, no award-winning performances from you?"

"Nope. I was the perfect child."

He chuckled, casting a quick glance toward the Christmas tree where Jeremy lay, still soundly asleep. "No way. Didn't we establish that you were pretty wild? You probably gave your mother premature gray hair and an ulcer to boot."

Shannon felt her smile become fixed and she nearly tossed out a smart remark, agreeing to Alex's assessment. But he needed to be reassured that Jeremy would be all right.

"The truth is that after my father…when we lost him, I kept things bottled up." She rubbed the back of her neck, searching for an explanation she'd never voiced aloud. "We all reacted in our own way, and I decided to be the one who didn't cause trouble."

"Shannon, please. You don't have to talk about it."

"I don't mind." She grinned wryly. "Actually, I *do* mind, but that's okay. Dad was killed in an accident working for a lumber company. After it happened, I never let anyone know how I felt, or how much I hurt…about anything.

I'd say something clever or tease or make a joke, but I wouldn't cry or make anyone sad. That was my idea of not making trouble."

"That meant you were all alone."

Startled, Shannon gazed quickly at Alex. He sounded appalled, but he also understood. In a house filled with her mother and brothers and sisters, she'd been alone.

She shivered and drew back. She hadn't intended to strip her soul bare, but that was how she felt.

"It wasn't so bad," she said in instinctive denial. "The point is, I got through it, and I didn't turn out to be such a horrible person, did I?"

"Not horrible at all."

"And with some time and a lot of love, I'm sure Jeremy will be all right, too."

Alex swirled the cola in his glass. Shannon hadn't said anything new, but it meant more coming from her. She'd been there, gone through what Jeremy was going through, and she had seen her brothers and sisters go through it as well.

"Then you're saying I shouldn't worry."

She gave him a quick smile. "Of course you're going to worry. You're his daddy. My mom says worry is in a parent's job description."

He liked the way she said *daddy*. Not *father* or *parent*, but *daddy*. Any man could father a child; not all of them were daddies. His own father was the perfect example—a man with so many personal problems, he didn't have energy to think about the kids he'd helped create.

"I'm no expert," Shannon murmured, "but I called my mother and talked to her after picking up Jeremy. I know you've been concerned, and thought she might have some advice. After all, she raised nine children and we all lived to tell about it."

"I don't think I could handle nine. Just having one has me overwhelmed."

"You might surprise yourself. Mom says it doesn't get easier with each child, but you become more shock-resistant."

"She sounds smart. Maybe she can tell me how to help a pregnant sixteen-year-old prodigy," he muttered, his mind unable to erase the memory of the fear in his young student's face, and the knowledge that something had irrevocably changed her life. No matter what Rita decided to do about her baby, it was something she'd live with forever.

"Sixteen?"

"Yes. That's why I asked if you'd pick up Jeremy. A member of the football team seduced her as part of an initiation challenge. She told me after class. She'd been crying…I couldn't leave without doing something."

"I'll kill him." Shannon's eyes flashed furiously.

"Get in line."

"I mean it, Alex. What's his name?"

"I mean it, too, but she wouldn't tell me his name." Alex gazed at Shannon's passionate expression, fascinated. He'd reacted to the situation as an intellectual, coolly, professionally, though he'd been outraged; Shannon's reaction was purely from the heart.

The philosophical concepts of yin and yang, opposites that complemented each other, crept into his mind.

No.

He surged to his feet.

"You've been terrific, but if Jeremy's really coming

down with something, then we're exposing you to his germs unnecessarily. I'd better get him home."

Her eyebrows shot upward. "What about your student?"

"She's with the counselors at the school health center. They're going to work with her. I shouldn't have said anything, but I wanted you to know there was a good reason I asked for your help," he said quickly.

It was a lie.

He'd told her because he'd needed to talk about the situation with someone else. It was odd, but the school counselors had frustrated him with their guarded responses. He was a careful man himself—a man who avoided emotion—yet he'd wanted to hear *someone* explode in outrage on Rita's behalf.

He leaned over his son. "It's time to go," he murmured.

Jeremy snuggled deeper into the pillow, so Alex lifted him in his arms.

"No, Daddy," came a sleepy murmur. "Wanna stay with Shannon."

Considering the magical toy train and marvelous Christmas tree, he wasn't surprised by Jeremy's response, yet a piercing ache went through Alex. He'd tried to get Jeremy interested in buying a tree, but his son had just sighed and said it wouldn't be like Shannon's. How a child could fall madly in love with someone in such a short time was beyond comprehension.

Shannon followed them to the door with Jeremy's jacket, and when Alex turned to say goodnight, he caught the faint scent of her perfume.

God, she smelled good.

He stared into her green eyes and felt unwelcome sensations, sensations that reminded him he was still alive, even if his wife was gone.

"Er…thanks again. For everything," he muttered, taking the jacket and tucking it around his son.

Without another word he opened the door and left before he could do something he'd regret.

Chapter Five

"I don't wanna babysitter," Jeremy declared, his small chin setting stubbornly.

Alex sighed. "We need someone for a few days. You can't go to day-care until we're sure you don't have strep throat."

"Not going back there, either. I want Shannon."

Blast.

Alex rubbed at his temples. He'd sat at Jeremy's bed-side most of the night, watching him breathe, gauging how sick he was getting. He'd enjoyed few restful nights since losing Kim, but it was his child's health that robbed him of sleep now.

He'd do anything for his son.

Did "anything" include Shannon O'Rourke?

Alex had cashed in her offer of help once already, but she handled Jeremy so well. By contrast, Jeremy was still convinced the day-care center meant Mr. Tibbles harm by trying to "poke" the rabbit with a needle.

"*Pleeeze,* Daddy. Mr. Tibbles likes Shannon."

The heartfelt plea was more than Alex could withstand. "All right, I'll talk to her," he said.

Feeling as if he was caught in a quagmire that was pulling him down no matter how hard he tried to escape it, Alex stepped outside and knocked on Shannon's door. He'd heard a few sounds from her side of their shared wall earlier that morning, so he figured she was awake.

When the door opened and he saw her, looking bright and beautiful as a new penny, he felt old and tired in comparison. For nearly a year he'd struggled, trying to make sense of his life and figure out how to be a father to a withdrawn, grieving child. Now Shannon had dropped into the picture, and she was like a forbidden Christmas ornament dangling from a branch, just beyond reach.

She represented a sweet escape from the struggle, but escape wasn't possible. He could only endure.

"Is Jeremy all right?" Shannon asked.

"Yeah. He's sniffling and has a sore throat, but it seems to be just a cold like you thought. The thing is, there's a lot of strep throat going around, and the day-care center wants me to wait a couple of days to rule it out before bringing him back. I do have a babysitter I could call, but Jeremy's being difficult and I—"

"If you want to know if I'll take care of him, the answer is yes," she said.

"Are you sure you don't mind? Watching a sick kid is a lousy way to use a vacation day. And there's more chance you'll catch his bug."

"I'm sure. Besides, I never get sick," Shannon said, at the same minute her brain was screaming in pure panic.

Taking care of a little boy for a whole day was a much bigger step than watching him for a couple of hours.

"That's great." Alex sounded as if he wasn't actually sure it was great, but he was saying so because he didn't have a choice.

His behavior irritated her. She wished she understood more about single fathers. Then she might know why Alex's face and posture said one thing, while his voice said another. If he really didn't want her to take care of Jeremy, why had he knocked on her door in the first place?

"I'm happy to spend the day with him," she said firmly.

"If he was worse, I'd stay home, only with finals next week it isn't a good time to miss class," he said.

Alex removed a key from his key ring and handed it to her, along with a business card. "Here's a key to my condo so you can spend the day there if you want. Feel free to use whatever you need. My office and cell phone numbers are on the card. I usually turn off the cell in class, but I'll leave it on today."

She glanced at the key and had a sudden burning urge to see the inside of the McKenzie household. Would it be neat? Disorganized? Would it still reflect the influence of Jeremy's mother, who had been the homebody sort who made everything nice? A vision of lace doilies and crocheted toilet-paper-roll covers went through her head—a dizzying image in the face of Alex's rugged masculinity.

"Er…I'll let Jeremy take the lead," she murmured.

Suddenly, Jeremy appeared under Alex's elbow and smiled up tremulously. "Is it okay, Daddy?"

"Yes. Go back inside, son, where it's warm."

"No. Go to Shannon's now."

Quick as a monkey, he scooted past his daddy, and Shannon instinctively crouched to catch him in a hug.

Oh…goodness.

A warm, fuzzy sensation curled in her tummy.

She glanced up at Alex and tingles of electricity gave her a different kind of warmth. Barefoot despite the cold, clad in faded jeans and a University of Washington sweatshirt, he had just the right blend of unconscious confidence and sex appeal to make a woman weak in the knees.

"You—" Her voice cracked and she cleared it.

Alex might be yummier than a chocolate sundae, but she wasn't interested.

Liar, screamed her conscience.

Why else would she keep from confessing that she couldn't boil water and didn't have a clue about kids?

Not for the first time she reminded herself that a relationship between them was doomed. He was a family man who loved primitive countries, and she was a city woman. Her idea of survival skills was knowing how to get rid of the containers that came with take-out food.

Straightening, she plastered a polite smile on her face. "Go ahead and get ready for work. Jeremy is fine here."

"Thanks." Alex's blue eyes darkened and a spasm of emotion crossed his face as he looked down at his son. He still hadn't shaved, but his shadow of a beard and rumpled appearance made him look even sexier. "I shouldn't be too late."

He turned and crossed their side-by-side driveways, then disappeared inside his condo.

Shannon breathed a sigh of relief and directed Jeremy into her house. The less time she spent with his daddy, the better for all of them.

* * *

After lunchtime had come and gone, Shannon was exhausted. But it wasn't a bad exhausted. A local store had agreed to deliver groceries—including their "home-made chicken noodle soup," guaranteed to cure colds "just like Mom's did." She'd only boiled a little over in the microwave while reheating it, so nothing disastrous had happened.

Afterward, Jeremy had talked her through making instant cocoa, before delightedly playing with the train again.

The doorbell rang, breaking into her thoughts, and she hurried into the other room, smiling at Jeremy who was curled up on the couch with a blanket.

He blinked sleepily at her. "S'Daddy," he predicted.

Sure enough, Alex McKenzie waited on the step with an anxious expression in his eyes. "Is Jeremy all right?"

"He's fine. I would have called if there was a problem."

Part of Alex's mind registered the annoyed tone in Shannon's voice, but the other part appreciated the dark green dress she wore. It was made of a soft fabric that clung like a second skin, and he itched to see how it might peel away. Was she wearing underwear? There weren't any obvious lines that—

Damn.

His thoughts were going in directions he'd sworn he wouldn't allow them to go. Shannon was a neighbor—nothing more. It was natural that after a year of being celibate certain feelings would return. And if he felt as if he was being unfaithful to Kim, then that was something he'd have to resolve within himself.

"How did it go?" he asked as Shannon invited him inside.

"Great. We got a few of his toys and books from next

door, and we read together, stuff like that. I think he's feeling a little better."

"Uh-uh," Jeremy declared immediately. "Not better. I wanna come back tomorrow."

He let out an unconvincing cough and Alex covered a smile. Mr. Tibbles lay on the floor, over ten feet away from Jeremy, sending a surge of joy through him. After the disaster at the day-care center, he'd worried that Jeremy would be more bonded than ever to the stuffed rabbit, but everything seemed to be all right.

"Maybe Shannon can tell us how to decorate our own Christmas tree," he said, trying to distract his determined son. "How about it, Shannon?"

Alex looked at Shannon in time to see another strange, altogether unreadable expression on her face. Honestly, how could a man have a prayer of figuring her out?

"I'll give you mine. That'll be easier," she said. "And the train set, of course. That way you can have a tree right away."

He'd expected anything from a polite "Sorry, I'm too busy," to an enthusiastic "Yes," but not such a generous offer.

He shook his head. "We couldn't do that."

"Daddy—"

"No, Jeremy, we can't take Shannon's tree. I know you like coming here because of the train and everything, but we have our own home."

Shannon stayed silent, lips pressed together as Alex collected Jeremy's things and said good-bye. Her eyes narrowed as the front door shut behind them, leaving her in silence.

I know you like coming here because of the train and everything...

Of all the insulting things to say.

Even if it was true, it was still rude. And it wasn't only

because of the Christmas tree and train set that Jeremy liked her. He'd liked her at the post office before they'd ever been inside her condo.

Shannon marched to the phone. Her family would think she was acting like a fool, but that was just too bad. She hadn't known what to say when Alex asked for help with a Christmas tree, so she'd panicked and offered to give them her own tree.

Now she had a plan.

"Miranda? It's Shannon. I have another job for you," she said when her sister answered, then settled down to explain what she wanted.

The next day, Shannon waited until after nine in the evening before carrying various boxes out of her house and stacking them near the McKenzies' front step.

She figured Alex was still awake since he seemed to be a night person. Lately she was even more aware of sounds on the other side of their shared wall. Bathwater ran every evening around eight, followed by rustles of noise in one of the smaller bedrooms—presumably Jeremy being put to bed. Later, long after she'd gone to bed herself, she'd hear muffled thuds and bumps and the sound of a shower from the master-bedroom suite that gradually quieted. Usually after midnight.

The lights were still on downstairs, so she tapped on the door and waited, stifling a yawn. Night was not her best time; she liked mornings.

"Shannon?" Alex said, swinging the door open. "Is something wrong?"

"Of course not. I have your tree." She motioned to the boxes her sister had brought to the condo earlier.

"What are you talking about?"

"You wanted my help with a Christmas tree, so here it is."

Alex blinked as Shannon grabbed a carton and pushed past him into the living room. He'd spent the evening listening to Jeremy chatter about Shannon, and couldn't he go to her home tomorrow instead of calling the babysitter again? His son had finally gone to sleep, and now here was Shannon. In the flesh, so to speak, clad in tight black jeans and a black sweater embroidered with green and silver holly leaves across the breast and all that glorious red hair...

He let out a harsh breath.

"Where do you want me?" she asked.

He thought of saying he wanted her in his king-size bed. Much as he didn't want to deal with those kinds of feelings, apparently he didn't have any choice. But he didn't have to act on them. He'd always prided himself on his self-control, determined to be different from his mother and father.

"I asked for advice on decorating a tree. I never thought you'd go out and buy something. How much do I owe you?"

She shrugged, her long hair glinting like fire. "You don't owe me anything. This is a gift."

"I can't accept—"

"It isn't for you, it's a gift for Jeremy," she said coolly. "I'll set it up now, so he can be surprised in the morning when he wakes up."

She seemed edgy, as if filled with suppressed emotion, and he frowned. "Is something wrong?"

"Heavens, what could be wrong?"

Her smile, like her voice, exuded false cheerfulness. Something *was* wrong, but she wouldn't admit it. Moreover, he had the damnedest feeling she was furious.

With him.

What had he done?

Well…he had insulted her brother and generally tried to avoid her whenever he wasn't asking a favor, both of which were probably enough to infuriate most women. But why would she go to all this trouble if she was so mad at him?

They worked in silence, carrying boxes into the house and setting up the artificial tree.

"I prefer real evergreen, but artificial trees are safer," Shannon said as she tugged light strings around the branches. "Especially for children," she added. "They want the lights on all the time, which dries out a cut tree and creates a fire hazard." She sounded as if she was repeating something from a book, or something she'd heard.

It took awhile, but gradually the tree was decorated so it resembled a child's toyland dream. Yet several boxes still remained, and when she unpacked the first two, he saw that they contained a toy train set that was far more elaborate than the one running around the base of Shannon's own tree.

"No," he said quietly. "I either pay for this, or you return it to the store."

"My brother is a generous employer. I can afford it."

"So can I."

"I told you before, it's a gift."

"Why? You hardly know us." Alex caught Shannon's arm and pulled her around to face him. He was stunned to see unshed tears in her deep green eyes. "What's going on?"

"You don't want Jeremy wanting to come see me, so obviously you have to have a better tree and train set. Then he won't want to come over and you can pretend we never met."

Shocked, he stared into her hurt eyes, realizing how it must have sounded to Shannon the night before when he was trying to get Jeremy to leave without fussing. He hadn't meant to suggest his son only wanted to visit her because of her tree and train. And he never would have imagined that Shannon O'Rourke, with her carefree smile and sophistication, would take his tactless words so hard.

But he should have guessed.

She'd told him that as a child she'd locked her hurt away, keeping it hidden from the world. It was obvious that she was still hiding the wounds and hurts from view.

"I didn't mean it, not like that," he said helplessly. "You've been great to Jeremy, and he really responds to you. It's just that we've been through so much and he's so little. He doesn't understand some things. I worry about him getting attached and hoping that something will happen between us."

"And that would be awful, wouldn't it? Getting involved with me?" Shannon asked, the words dripping with injured sarcasm. She busied herself lifting out the train and assembling pieces of track.

Damnation.

It was his own fault for saying something so easily misinterpreted. Still, maybe he *did* want Shannon's Christmas tree to be the reason Jeremy wanted to go to her home so badly. He'd spent so much of his son's childhood in other parts of the world, then Kim had gotten sick, going so quickly, and he'd realized he had wasted three years. Three years when he could have been getting to know his own child. And now Jeremy would rather spend time with Shannon than with his own father.

"I'm not interested in getting married again, that's all," he murmured. "It has nothing to do with you."

"Of course not."

But her hurt look hadn't faded and he groaned silently. He didn't deal well with mixed signals and sensitive feelings. Even with his wife he'd struggled, and Kim had been exceptionally calm and good-natured. They'd rarely argued, and then only about Jeremy.

With Shannon it seemed as if all his nerve endings were exposed. He didn't know why, except she was alive and vibrant, and so obviously off-limits.

"You're beautiful, Shannon, you have to know that," Alex whispered.

"Beautiful." She tested the word as if she'd never heard it before. "What has that got to do with anything?"

"Nothing. Everything. I was just trying to be clear."

Shannon thought Alex was as clear as mud. She didn't even know why she was so stirred up over such an unreasonable man. At her request, Miranda had spent half the day collecting ornaments and specialty items for that darned Christmas tree, and the second half showing Shannon how to properly decorate it.

She had it so bad for Alex, she hadn't even tried to make light of things with her sister. She'd tersely explained the decorations were for her next-door neighbor and his little boy, and to please not ask any questions. By now everyone in the O'Rourke family would know she'd gone around the bend. They would tease and tease, and she'd toss her head and give it right back to them.

Her feelings didn't get hurt.

She was too tough for that. Her heart might have gotten broken when she was younger, but at twenty-eight she'd seen enough of the world to know better.

Right.

And Santa Claus was going to climb down her chimney on Christmas Eve.

"These are stockings for the mantel," she said, getting up quickly.

The mantel didn't have anything on it. For that matter, aside from Jeremy's bedroom, the inside of the condo was generally bleak, with only toys and books adding color to the off-white walls and beige furniture. She arranged the two stockings on their hooks, then stepped back and bumped into Alex.

"Sorry," she muttered, jerking away as every atom in her body reacted to the contact.

Leaning down, she collected a garland of silk holly leaves and berries and arranged it on the mantel, then put two battery-operated candle lights on one end. With her sister's design, Alex McKenzie's living room looked quite festive.

"How's that?" she asked.

When he didn't say anything, she dusted her hands. "Guess I'd better get out of your way. You can finish putting the train together later."

Before she could do something stupid like cry, she headed in a beeline for the door. She had it open a few inches when Alex's hand slapped it shut, his breath coming raggedly as he arched over her. She twisted in the small space between him and the door and looked up.

Blue eyes, dark as a midnight sky, gazed down at her, eyes filled with regret and frustration…and heat.

"You get to me," he said harshly. "You must know that. You're a sexy woman and I haven't been with anyone for over a year. But I can't get involved with my next-door neighbor, not with my son looking on. Particularly when I don't plan to get married again. Do you understand?"

Despite Alex's declaration, she felt the hard bulge at the top of his thighs as he leaned into her. There seemed little difference between the muscled length of his body and the unyielding door, and an answering warmth radiated out from Shannon's breasts.

Her arms found their way around his neck and bubbles seemed to be sliding through her veins instead of blood.

"I understand," she said, though it wasn't true.

Alex's hand cupped her chin, and he pressed a kiss to her mouth, his tongue thrusting boldly inside, claiming her as easily as he breathed.

Shannon's moan was lost in the dark, hot joining. It had never been like this with another man, so out-of-control, so improper, so very good. His thumb rubbed across her nipple, then the world spun and there was a sensation of going down, of weight descending on her. She squirmed, inviting it.

He shoved her sweater and bra out of the way and his hands closed over her breasts with a hungry demand. She arched into the caress. Suddenly, Alex froze…and a second later she knew the reason. From the second floor came the faint sound of coughing.

Alex stared at her as she breathed in deep gasps, trying to clear her head. His eyes darkened, his gaze lingering on the sensitive peaks of her breasts. Her nipples tightened as if they'd been stroked and a low moan rose from her throat. She couldn't remember the last time she had felt anything close to the way he was making her feel.

"Daddy?" Jeremy called in the silence, still sounding hoarse from his cold. "Can I have a drink of water?"

"Stay where you are," Alex ordered hastily. "I'll be right up."

Finally coming to her senses, Shannon bolted upright and yanked her clothing into place. Her first thought was escape, but Alex put a hand on her arm as she scrambled to her feet.

"You stay, too," he said. "We have to talk."

Chapter Six

What a mess.

Shannon sat on the floor, blindly assembling the toy train she'd brought, and tried to understand why she'd let Alex kiss her like that.

Because you *wanted* to kiss him, that's why, you idiot, her conscience taunted, and she rolled her eyes. Kissing Alex was a lost cause. He'd made it clear he wasn't getting married again, and she was tired of being single and pretending to like it.

The O'Rourkes were marrying kind of people.

Even Neil had accepted the truth, and sooner or later her youngest brother and three sisters would find their soul mates, as well. The brides would toss their bouquets and they'd go on their honeymoons and start their families. She was happy for them, but it was hard feeling left behind.

She wanted to believe she had a soul mate, too, but she'd stubbed her romantic toes too many times to have much hope of finding someone to love her as she was, domestic limitations and all.

Face grim, Alex walked down the staircase and sat on the bottom step. He didn't say anything and Shannon tried to calm her queasiness. Was he angry, blaming her for that brief moment when the needs of his body had outweighed the caution in his mind?

Taking a deep breath, she squared her shoulders. "Aren't you glad we got that out of our systems?" Her voice cracked a couple of times, but it was the best quip she could devise in her current state of mind.

"Did we?"

Her eyes narrowed.

If Alex said something chauvinistic or crude, she was going to kick him. "At least you could pretend."

He sighed. "I'm not good at pretending, Shannon. I spent my childhood in a marital war zone, followed by divorced-parent hell, never knowing when the screaming was going to start. I got lucky with Kim, but I don't expect to get lucky a second time. That's just one of the reasons I'm not getting married again."

"I don't remember asking you to marry me."

"I can't have an affair, either. It's nothing against you, but I have to think about Jeremy."

Shannon glared. The male half of the human race was so arrogant, she didn't know why women bothered with them. "That's fine, because I *also* didn't ask you for an affair. Have you forgotten I was leaving when you stopped me? Besides, it was just a kiss."

"I'm not so sure." Alex let out a low curse. "This isn't going to work. I can't let Jeremy start hoping for something that isn't going to happen."

"What isn't going to work? We're agreed we aren't getting married, and we aren't having an affair. So I wouldn't worry about Jeremy getting his hopes up about anything."

"You heard him that first night." He gave her a moody look. *"If Shannon was my new mommy, we could eat pizza whenever we wanted."*

Shannon sighed. Even *she* knew children said things they didn't understand. "That was just wishful thinking. It surprised me, but he would have said the same thing to a ninety-five-year-old grandmother who suggested pizza for dinner."

A faint smile pulled at Alex's mouth. "Ninety-five?"

"Yes. You don't actually think Jeremy knows why people get married, do you? He's too young for that."

"I should hope he doesn't," Alex said fervently. He had a sudden vision of trying to explain the birds and bees to Jeremy in a few years. It was enough to turn him gray. With his luck, his precocious little boy would start noticing girls by the time he was five.

Shannon chuckled and he looked at her. "What's so funny?"

"You look as if you're contemplating a snake-infested swamp."

"Worse, I was imagining having to explain sex to my son. It's pure luck that I'm not explaining it right now. The modified version, of course."

"Of course." She laughed harder, and after a moment he grinned, as well. There was nothing coy or shy about Shannon and it was surprisingly refreshing.

"Hey, someday you'll be in my shoes and it won't seem so funny."

"Maybe, but it's further away in my future."

"Don't you want kids?"

Her smile faltered. "One day. Maybe." She began working on the train again and he sat next to her, fitting pieces together, as well. The town took shape, along with a small forest of trees and a mountain with a tunnel.

He sighed. "You were supposed to take this back. And here I am, helping put it together."

"Call it a permanent loan. I don't need two toy trains."

He opened his mouth, then closed it again, instead snapping together the last piece of track. Jeremy would love the tree and train, but he doubted his son would talk less about Shannon just because they now had their own Christmas wonderland.

There was something about Shannon that was hard to forget. The more Alex saw of her, the less he saw the breezy sophisticate from their first meeting. He wasn't sure if that was good or bad, because the woman beneath the surface was intelligent, charming…and ever so appealing.

It was baffling, but he just plain *liked* Shannon. She was far too emotional, something he'd always avoided in both male and female friends. And he would have expected her to act like a spoiled princess given her family's wealth, but she was down-to-earth and generous to a fault. It made him uncomfortable in ways he hadn't expected, raising questions about the way he'd lived, the way he'd denied the deeper workings of his own soul.

The train's power cords were hidden from view and Shannon flipped a switch on the control board. The lights of the Victorian town twinkled merrily beneath the tree.

"How's that?" she asked.

"It's great. You have a gift for this sort of thing."

She had a gift for handling public relations problems,

not decorating or cooking. But she could write a check and wield a credit card with the best homemaker on the planet.

"My sister is responsible," she admitted. "Miranda is a professional decorator, and she had most of this stuff in stock already. Anything you want, she can take care of."

"Can she take care of my big mouth?" Alex rubbed the back of his neck. "Please believe me, I never meant to hurt your feelings yesterday. The truth is, I was jealous. Jeremy is the most important thing in the world to me, yet you've been able to reach him, when I can't."

The pain in Alex's face turned Shannon's stomach into mush. "You mustn't worry, he adores you," she whispered.

His mouth lifted in a brief smile. "I appreciate that, but I still can't reach him. Why, Shannon? Why can't I get through to my own son?"

She thought about her day with Jeremy, and the quick, almost guilty look he'd given his father when he had said he couldn't remember his mother's face.

"Maybe he's trying to protect you," she said gently.

"Protect *me?* What are you talking about?"

Shannon let out a breath and wondered if she was mistaken. Her instincts told her she was right, but her instincts might be wrong. Still…

"The thing is…I don't see any pictures or keepsakes of your wife around, and you seem reluctant to talk about her in front of Jeremy. Maybe he's decided it hurts you too much, and he's trying not to upset you." She lifted her shoulders in a shrug. "Problem is, those feelings don't go away."

"He's a child. I'm supposed to take care of him."

"Yes, but when someone dies, people say odd things. Things like 'smile.' 'Don't be so sad.' 'Be strong for your family. For your mommy. For your daddy.'"

"Damn." Alex rubbed his face, his mind working furiously.

Could that be it?

Jeremy thinking he had to grieve in silence…the way Shannon had grieved? He gazed at her and wondered what other secrets were hidden behind her green eyes and bright smiles.

"Somebody said that to you, didn't they?" he murmured.

She shrugged noncommittally. "Isn't it strange that people tell you not to be sad when you've lost someone? Why shouldn't you be sad when that happens?"

A long sigh came from Alex's diaphragm.

Shannon scared the hell out of him, but he was also starting to understand how seductive powerful emotions could be. Time after time, his parents had torn each other to pieces. They should have called it quits after their first knock-down-drag-out fight, but neither one of them had been able to leave, not for fourteen years.

And he'd bet that a man, once hooked, wouldn't be able to leave Shannon any longer than it took to turn off the lights and pull her close.

"What are you thinking?" she whispered, and Alex fought the appeal of her sweet concern.

He inhaled sharply…a mistake.

His senses were filled with the subtle perfume of her skin, a scent that teased and tempted. He'd prided himself on his control, determined to be different from his parents, but now that control was vanishing.

Alex closed his eyes and tried to summon Kim's image, but all that came was a twinge of guilt and the warmth of a cherished memory.

No. He clenched his fists in denial. He didn't relish the

role of grieving widower, but Kim had deserved better than a husband who spent most of his nights in a foreign clime. At the very least she deserved a man who grieved for her properly.

"Shannon…we changed the subject, but nothing has actually changed," he forced himself to say. "Seeing you isn't good for me. Truly, it's my problem. You're terrific, but I don't want to be involved with anyone. Jeremy has to come first."

Shannon looked down, her heart aching for a thousand different reasons. She'd been drawn to Alex from the beginning, and it hurt to have him push her away. But some things were more important than her feelings.

"I agree that Jeremy comes first," she said quietly. "But you said yourself that I've been able to reach him. Are you willing to throw that away? We can make it clear that we're just friends. And we can make sure it stays that way when we're alone," she added.

Alex was silent for so long she wondered if he'd heard, or was thinking some dark thoughts of his own. Then his eyebrows lifted. "Friends? After what just happened?"

"Men and women can be friends without sex and romance coming into it," she said, exasperated. She had good male friends. And while she'd never tried to be friends with a man she found as attractive as Alex, it had to be possible. Her brother, Dylan, had been buddies with Kate Douglas since they were kids before he'd finally woken up and married her.

Swell.

Shannon shook her head in disgust.

Dylan and Kate were *not* a good example. But she was still certain it could be done.

"We'll just have to work at it," she said.

"All right," Alex agreed slowly, though he didn't seem a hundred-percent convinced.

"Good. I'm still off work, so if you need someone to sit with Jeremy, I'm available."

"That would be great."

She stuck her hand out and they shook, a silly formality that should have made her laugh. But it was hard to laugh around the lump in her throat, or the tears trying to find their way to the surface once again.

"How's that, Jeremy?"

Jeremy solemnly regarded the cup of flour Shannon held up. "It's s'posed to be at the line."

"Oh. Right." She scooped some flour from the measuring cup and shook it a little. "Is that better?"

"Okay."

She dumped the flour into the bowl with the other dry ingredients and gave the mixture a dubious look. The cookbook she'd bought claimed this was a foolproof recipe for gingerbread cookies, but she had her doubts. Nobody had Shannon-O'Rourke-proofed a recipe yet.

At least her agreement to be "just friends" with Alex meant she didn't have to worry about him discovering she was the domestic equivalent of a shipwreck. On the other hand, she still hadn't rushed to tell him the truth, either, particularly when he'd asked if she'd make cookies with Jeremy.

The words had stuck in her throat.

Instead of saying, "Sorry, but I couldn't bake a cookie to save my life," she'd agreed to his request. Worst of all, she and Jeremy were making those cookies in the McKenzie kitchen, rather than her house, so anything she broke, spindled or mutilated would belong to Alex. Fortunately, he was upstairs, looking for something, instead of sitting in the kitchen watching her make a fool of herself. But sooner or later he'd come down and see her mess up the place.

At least Jeremy looked content. He had smudges of flour on his cheeks and a smile on his mouth; it was worth a little humiliation if it made him happy. And he was so smart. He could already read words like *flour* and *sugar* and *ginger,* and he understood measurements.

He was *also* smart enough to understand the difference between really being sick, and pretending because he didn't like the changes in his life.

"Jeremy, have you ever heard the story about the boy who cried wolf?" she asked casually.

He shook his head. "Uh-uh."

"It's about a little boy who was given the job of watching the sheep for his village. A village is a small town," she explained. "It was an important job, making sure a wolf didn't come and scare the animals."

"What was the boy's name?"

Shannon blinked and thought furiously. She didn't know the story that well, just the highlights and the message behind it. "I think…I think his name was…Bob." She cringed the moment the name came from her mouth, but she was new to this storytelling thing.

"Bob?"

"Y-yes. Bobby. Bobby liked watching the sheep, but sometimes it was boring, and he wanted to get the villagers' attention. So he'd cry 'Wolf!' and everyone would drop what they were doing and come to help chase it away. But when they got there, he'd laugh because they were out of breath and worried, and *he* knew it was just a joke."

Jeremy darted a look at her. "That wasn't nice."

"You're right, it wasn't nice. Unfortunately, he kept doing it and the villagers stopped believing him. Then one day a wolf *did* come."

"What did he do?"

She swallowed, suddenly unsure of herself. A sheep-eating wolf was a grim tale for a four year old; it might have been better if she'd asked Alex before starting the story.

"Uh…Bobby called, but no one came from the village."

This time Jeremy didn't even look at her; he just nodded.

"Do you understand why it was so important for Bobby to tell the truth?" she asked, brushing some of the flour from his cheek. "It's like when you say you're sick, except you really just want to see your daddy. After a while nobody knows if anything is really wrong."

Jeremy's small lower lip pouted out, then a huge sigh rose from him. "But I don't like day-care." He planted his elbows on the table and looked angry. "Why did Mommy have to go away?"

Her chest tightened. He'd gone right to the tough question, the question she'd asked so many times about her own father.

"I don't know…but I know that she didn't want to leave you." Shannon pushed the bowl of flour and other ingredients to one side and sat next to him. Some things were more important than cookies. "Tell me about your mommy."

Standing outside the kitchen, Alex fought a thousand different emotions as he listened to Shannon. Pain at the emptiness Kim's death had left, love for the woman who'd been his wife…anger at life's injustices.

And hope, hearing Shannon encourage Jeremy to talk.

Soon his son was pouring out stories about Mommy taking him to the pond to sail paper boats, about cookies and bedtime stories, and the songs she used to sing. Things Alex had thought Jeremy was too young to remember, but which had actually been carefully guarded in his heart.

Alex looked down at the picture he'd unearthed from storage in the attic, one of the rare photos taken of him, Kim and Jeremy as a family. And beneath it was another of Kim with her swollen tummy, proud and happy, just days before giving birth to a healthy baby boy.

He had to wonder if he'd hidden the pictures away to protect himself, when he'd believed he was doing the right thing for Jeremy. How long could you deny feelings you simply didn't want to accept?

"I bet it was funny when your mother dressed up like that," Shannon said in the other room.

Alex's eyes widened as Jeremy giggled. "Mommy drew whiskers on her face and wiggled her nose. Just like a kitty."

Halloween.

Kim had been terribly sick by then, but she'd made them laugh when she'd donned cat's ears and painted her cheeks. She'd been determined to make it through the holidays, to spend that special time with her "men." How could he have forgotten those moments when she'd pushed the dread away and let them be a family?

Fighting the tightness in his throat, Alex stepped into the kitchen and looked at Jeremy, smiling and happy, the shadows chased from his eyes as he talked about the things that he'd loved about his mommy.

Gratitude filled Alex as he turned his gaze to Shannon. He felt the inevitable throb of desire as well, but he didn't mind it as much as usual. He'd never believed in divine intervention, yet Shannon's fortuitous entry into their lives was enough to make him wonder about the possibility.

"Jeremy, I thought you'd like to have some pictures of your mother," he said, determined to continue the good his beautiful neighbor had started. "You're in this one." He sat at the table and showed his son the one of a very pregnant Kim.

"That's not me, that's just Mommy," Jeremy denied, but he gazed at the photo with growing delight.

"Nope." Alex pointed to the bulge in Kim's tummy. "That's you, a few days before you were born. And you're the reason she's smiling. You made your mommy so very happy."

He glanced at Shannon over his son's head and wished he could tell her how he felt, but gratitude was mixed with other feelings, less easy to understand.

She challenged him.

Somehow he knew it was because of Shannon that he'd listened to his distraught student, instead of avoiding the tears in her reddened eyes, the way he always avoided emotional scenes. It wasn't that he didn't care about people, but it was easier to give money than get involved.

Shannon had gotten involved with his son because she knew what it was like to lose a parent and was willing to open that old hurt to help a child she barely knew.

"How about pizza for dinner?" he asked, his gaze still fixed on Shannon. "We'll go over to that new Italian place that everyone says is so good."

"Yummy," Jeremy exclaimed.

"Shannon?" Alex prompted when she didn't say anything.

She nudged the bowl on the table. "What about the cookies?"

"Finish them tomorrow. Unless you're tired of us and want some time off."

"If I get tired of you, you'll know it," she said, giving him one of her exasperated looks.

"Let's go then." It seemed only natural to put out his hand and she took it with a questioning smile. When she stood, he was surprised to see the top of her head only came to his shoulder. He kept thinking of Shannon as tall, but it was an illusion of her leggy beauty and vibrant nature.

They were friends, Alex reminded himself. Her height—or lack of it—wasn't something he should be thinking about.

"You put on your coats. I'll start the Jeep and get the heat going," he said quickly.

"All right."

Outside, he saw that clouds had rolled across the Puget Sound area. A misting rain drizzled through the twilight, so fine it was like fog shrouding the landscape. The windows clouded up the moment he got inside the Jeep, and it took several minutes before warm air began coming through the vents.

"I don't know about this. Maybe you'd prefer staying in," he said when he'd returned inside his condo. "It's a miserable night."

Shannon smiled. "I don't mind, if you don't. This is Christmas weather."

His eyebrows shot upward. "Snow is Christmas weather. This is just cold and wet."

"Give it a chance. We don't get many white Christmases in this part of the country, but there's the smell of wood smoke and fresh-washed evergreen in the air, and all those strings of lights sparkle through the rain like tiny jewels."

Alex shook his head, yet when they walked outside to the waiting Jeep, he realized that the scent of wood smoke and evergreens did fill the air, and the early twilight was indeed brightened by the Christmas lights strung on trees and bushes and houses. He'd deliberately chosen a place that was different than their old home in Minnesota, but while they probably wouldn't have snow for Christmas, they'd have stands of pine and cedar keeping the forest green.

And they'd have Shannon.

The errant thought shook him. Desire was one thing, but he didn't want to need anyone...the kind of needing that tied your heart in knots and made good-byes so terrible.

"You're quiet all of a sudden," Shannon commented as he pulled out of the driveway. "Is something wrong?"

Alex summoned a smile. Shannon was a nice woman, and she was doing a lot for his son, but that didn't mean he needed her. He had to get a grip.

"Nothing's wrong. I just hadn't realized we wouldn't have a white Christmas."

"Well, we *might* get some early snow, but we usually don't before January. Even then it's iffy, and doesn't stay long on the ground unless an arctic storm comes down from Canada."

Using the discipline he'd honed over the years, Alex forced his brain into less disturbing directions.

Snow was a perfect distraction.

He mentally noted where he'd stored the snow shovel, and calculated how long it would take to shovel the walks and their two driveways. He'd shovel snow for any neighbor, so it wasn't significant that he planned to deal with Shannon's snow.

They were friends, weren't they?

Chapter Seven

Alex doggedly read the term papers piled on his desk and tried to ignore the cheerful sounds rising from the first floor of the condominium.

Jeremy hadn't forgotten about the half-finished cookies, and at 5:00 a.m. his son had been standing by his bed, asking if they could call Shannon to come and help finish making the "ginger people."

"You mean gingerbread men," he'd said groggily.

"Shannon says they're ginger people."

"Did she say ginger*bread* people?" Alex was never at his best in the morning, and getting into a semantics discussion with a four year old before the crack of dawn hadn't been the brightest idea in the world.

"Shannon says ginger people."

Of course. Whatever Shannon said was the gospel truth as far as Jeremy was concerned. It didn't matter, anyway. In the end they were just cookies.

"Okay," he'd muttered.

"Goody." His son had picked up the phone receiver and pushed it into Alex's hand. "Call now, Daddy."

Oh, God.

Why couldn't children sleep when other people were sleeping?

"Son, I didn't mean it was okay to call. I meant okay, they're ginger people."

"But, *Daddy*—"

"You don't want to wake Shannon up, do you? She's on vacation. Besides, you don't call friends this early in the morning."

Jeremy had reluctantly agreed, then he'd crawled into bed with him and talked for three straight hours, with liberal references to their neighbor and the things she'd done and said when they were together.

So much for his *daddy* sleeping late. Alex had finally given up and called Shannon at a more reasonable hour about the cookies. She'd come over looking fresh and wide-awake, while he felt like Grumpy and Sleepy from the Seven Dwarves rolled into one.

Conceding defeat, Alex abandoned the term papers and walked downstairs. His son and his neighbor were lying on their backs by the Christmas tree, holding kaleidoscopes in front of their eyes as cheerful Christmas carols played in the background. He smiled at the scene.

Shannon's auburn hair tumbled about her head and her knees swayed in time with the music. Her feet were bare, toenails painted pink. Snug jeans that showcased her legs were topped by a T-shirt with the words, Dear Santa, Just bring the five gold rings, printed on it. She looked like an unruly teenager, though he knew she must be in her late twenties.

Next to her was Jeremy, singing "Jingle Bells" off-key.

Mr. Tibbles wasn't anywhere in sight.

"Hey, I thought you were baking cookies," Alex said, his grin broadening.

"The dough has to chill before we roll it out," Shannon explained without looking up. She spun the dial on the end of the kaleidoscope and whistled a few notes in tune to the stereo. "I thought you were grading term papers."

"I'm taking a break."

"You ready for the final exams?"

"Yes. And I've been trying to work out a time for a makeup session, if the student has a good excuse."

Shannon sat up. "Really? I never heard of a professor willing to have a makeup session."

"Yeah? You couldn't charm them into it?" His comment felt dangerously like flirting, but it was hard to believe Shannon O'Rourke failing at anything she might go after.

"I never needed a makeup test. I was the perfect student."

"How perfect? No-skinny-dipping-in-Lake-Washington-during-Christmas-break perfect? Or grade-and-attendance perfect? There are different levels of perfect, you know. Some students are more perfect than others."

She laughed. "Nobody in their right mind skinny-dips in Lake Washington in December. Of course, one of my brothers did it, but he was crazy."

"What's 'kinny-dipping?" Jeremy asked.

Alex stifled a groan. He had a big mouth, and he obviously didn't know how to guard what he said around his own son. Jeremy was smart and precocious and he understood things far too well for comfort.

"Skinny-dipping is going swimming without your bathing suit," Shannon explained. "It sounds like more fun than it really is, especially when it's cold."

"Okay." Jeremy rolled over onto his stomach and started the toy train chugging around the tracks.

Alex sighed. Why was it so easy when Shannon explained something like that, and so difficult when he tried? Their gazes met and another grin curved his mouth at the merry humor in her eyes. In another life he would have thought it was funny as well, watching a parent squirm over the innocent things a child asked...and the loaded answers that followed.

He wanted to promise retribution, because it was guaranteed that Shannon O'Rourke's children would be a wild handful. But he bit his tongue, remembering her reaction the last time he'd said something about her having kids— a faltering smile and a flicker of unhappiness. He didn't want to spoil the moment.

"I need some coffee," he said, a yawn splitting his mouth. "How about you?"

"Sure."

In the kitchen Shannon sat and watched as Alex filled the coffeemaker with water. His hair was rumpled and his eyes sleepy. She didn't doubt that if it wasn't for Jeremy and term papers to grade, he'd still have his face stuffed in a pillow; he definitely wasn't a morning person.

Lord, she'd been up since before six, writing memos, responding to e-mails from the office...and sending a message to Kane that she wouldn't be at work for another week or two. He'd wonder about it, particularly since she'd just begged him to end her forced vacation, but it didn't matter. She was having too much fun.

Fun?

Shannon smothered a chuckle. Playing with Jeremy and trying to figure out how to bake cookies weren't her usual ideas of fun. Her family would die of shock if they discovered how she'd been spending her days. Her reputation as a disaster in the kitchen had reached epic proportions, a reputation that had spread to the office after she'd twice set fire to the break-room microwave.

"You have that devilish twinkle in your eyes. Promise you aren't laughing at me," Alex said, plunking two steaming mugs of coffee on the table. He dropped into a chair with a groan.

"Why would I laugh?"

"I open my mouth in front of my son and dumb things come out. Like mentioning skinny-dipping." Beard stubble rasped beneath his fingers as he rubbed his jaw and yawned again.

"Didn't you get any sleep last night?"

"Not enough. Jeremy decided that 5:00 a.m. was the perfect time to start making gingerbread men. Only he insists they're called ginger people, because that's what you call them."

Shannon dangled the cookie cutters she'd bought in front of Alex. "There are two sexes. I don't want to be exclusive. Besides, I have a politically correct cookbook that calls them ginger people."

He lifted one eyelid and glared at her. "Next time, I'm teaching him how to dial the phone so he can wake *you* up in the middle of the night."

"Five isn't the middle of the night."

"I knew it. You're one of *those* people, aren't you?"

"If you mean a morning person, the answer is yes."

"I mean one of those people who wakes up early and

thinks it's the best time of the day." He made a disgusted sound and gulped his coffee, yelping a second later, "That's hot!"

Shannon couldn't help herself, she dissolved into laughter. "You just made it, what would you think it is?"

Alex leaned back in his chair, regarding her. "Aren't you going to mother me? Where's the usual feminine sympathy like running to get an ice cube for my burned tongue?"

"Do you want to be mothered?"

"No."

"Then I'm not going to do that."

An odd gleam entered his eyes. "I think I'm going to like being friends with you, Shannon."

That was a switch. Alex had only agreed to a friendship for Jeremy's sake. Shannon swallowed a stab of regret and told herself to be grateful he'd agreed to anything. He was proof that her luck in the romance department hadn't changed.

She sipped her coffee and thought about the men she'd dated over the years. Some had hoped to get close to her wealthy brother through her. Others had been allergic to marriage or, on the flip side, had secretly wanted a perfect homemaker for a wife. Few of those had been as callous as her college love, who'd decided he couldn't handle her lack of homemaking skills and made sure their mutual friends knew exactly why they'd broken up.

She'd forced herself to joke about the split, but she'd died inside each time she laughed about the end of her first love.

"Are you asleep, too?"

Startled, Shannon lifted her head. Alex had leaned forward and seemed wider awake now that he'd burned his tongue and gotten more caffeine into his system.

"No, not asleep. But your coffee could put hair on my chest."

"Too strong for you?"

Her pulse jumped, but it had nothing to do with coffee, just the tug of her heart. If she wasn't careful, she could risk having it broken again, and she wasn't certain how many times a broken heart could heal.

"It's a little strong."

"I assumed morning people lived on coffee."

"Not me, but I can't speak for all morning people."

Shannon traced a circle on the table and tried to regain the peace she'd felt lying next to Jeremy, rediscovering the beauty of light and color captured in a kaleidoscope. How long had it been since she'd felt at peace? Children seemed to have a marvelous gift of simplicity, a way of cutting through the chaos of the world.

"Do you have something against being mothered?" she asked idly. She'd been thinking about inviting Alex and Jeremy to her family's Christmas celebration, and Pegeen O'Rourke mothered anyone who would let her.

"I'm an adult, I don't need mothering."

"Don't tell my mom that. I think she secretly wishes we'd never grown up, though she probably doesn't mind as much now that she has grandchildren to spoil."

"She sounds nice."

"Thanks. She is." Shannon didn't ask about Alex's mother, remembering how he'd described his childhood—*a marital war zone followed by divorced-parent hell.* Given his experience, he must have loved his wife beyond belief to have risked getting married.

Sorrow crowded Shannon's throat—sorrow for what Alex had lost, and what she might never have.

"I think that cookie dough must be cold enough," she said huskily. "And you have term papers to grade."

"Cracking the proverbial whip, huh?"

"Sure, that's what friends do."

Alex smiled and rose. "About the mothering," he said, "don't get the wrong idea. I've just had my fill of women rushing in and trying to take Kim's place."

"They probably mean well."

"Maybe. But I like your style better."

He sauntered out and Shannon shook her head. He liked her style. What did that mean? Maybe it didn't mean anything. Men thought they were direct and to the point, but they were beyond confusing.

"Jeremy?" she called. "How about making those ginger people now?"

Alex studied the term paper in front of him. He was trying to figure out a reason not to flunk the author, when the smell of something burning crept into his consciousness.

At almost the same moment the smoke alarm screeched and he jumped to his feet.

"Shannon?"

He raced downstairs, grabbing a fire extinguisher on the way. Smoke filled the kitchen, with the thickest billows rising from the stove and sink.

"It's…" Shannon coughed. "Everything is under control. Yeow!" She dumped a blackened cookie sheet into the sink and began flapping a dish towel.

As a precaution, Alex sprayed the smoking mess with the fire extinguisher, then grabbed Shannon and Jeremy and shoved them out the back door.

"Stay there," he ordered.

Inside, he opened windows, started the exhaust fans blowing and turned off the oven. When he was certain nothing was actually on fire, he put a cap over the smoke alarm to silence it. The sound of Christmas music replaced the shrill screech.

"It's all right now," he said, stepping into the backyard again.

Shannon had her arms wrapped around Jeremy, keeping him warm. She was shaking from the cold and he swore beneath his breath, realizing he'd overreacted when he'd shoved them outside. But when it was his family involved, he couldn't take any chances.

"Come back in, the smoke is nearly gone." Alex put out his hand and she released Jeremy.

"Go inside where it's warm," she said, her voice shaking.

Jeremy skipped through the door, but Shannon remained on the garden bench.

"Shannon?"

"I think I'll go home," she whispered.

He frowned. "Why?"

"It's better if I do." She blinked and a tear dripped down her cheek.

Damn. He wasn't good at this sort of thing, especially when he couldn't see any reason for her to be so upset. So some cookies got burned, it wasn't a disaster. On the other hand, he had a strange feeling that if he let Shannon leave, she wouldn't come back. And that *would* be a disaster, for reasons Alex didn't want to think about.

"Better how?"

"Just better." She swallowed hard and two more tears spilled over. "I'm sorry about the cookies. I should have told you that I can't cook, but I thought if I paid attention it would be all right."

She jumped up and rushed across the empty flower bed separating their small yards.

Oh, man. This was exactly the type of situation Alex hated dealing with the most. And if any other woman had cried over a burned tray of cookies he would have been exasperated, but it obviously meant something significant to Shannon.

"Shannon, don't go."

"It's really...*better*."

Shannon pulled at her sliding-glass door, but the dumb thing was locked. So much for a speedy exit. She spun around, not wanting to see Alex's face and the disappointment that must be there, but not having a choice.

"Hey, it's all right." He put his arms around her, warmth radiating from his body.

It was nice.

Strength and heat and comfort. She'd ached after their brief kiss, ached for a deeper touch, and the kind of tender holding that only came in her dreams. She'd wondered if Alex could be the man in those dreams, but it was useless to think that way. He'd pushed her away from the moment they met; the barriers around his heart were higher than the castle walls in any fairy tale.

"It's not okay." She sniffed, the scent of burned gingerbread mixed with his masculine scent. "You have no idea. Maybe it doesn't matter to you because you don't want me, but it matters."

"God, Shannon, it isn't you I don't want."

She knew that tone. Or she thought she did. He was trying to be gentle and not hurt her feelings.

"It's all right. Don't worry about it. I'm not your problem," she said tiredly. In an hour she'd manage to get some perspective, but right now she felt as if she'd crashed into a brick wall. She hated failing at anything.

Alex leaned into her. "You aren't a problem at all," he breathed in her ear.

She knew that tone, too.

The husky murmur.

The suggestion of awareness.

A swollen heat burned against her abdomen and she swallowed. "Alex, this isn't—"

His mouth smothered her protest. She resisted for a split second, knowing he'd regret touching her the minute he came to his senses. But when his strong hands closed over her breasts, her own senses scattered.

His touch wasn't the least bit hesitant, and the bold, kneading strength of his fingers sent streamers of longing through more than her body. She felt him to her soul.

Knowing that Alex didn't feel so strongly about her cooled her response. Then his knee pressed between her legs and she lost touch with reality.

Her life had been spinning nowhere, but with Alex holding her, she had an anchor. Yet it was curious that an anchor would make her head whirl and her blood bubble like champagne.

Their tongues met, velvet on velvet, framed by the hard lines of his mouth.

The only other time she could remember a kiss being so good was when he'd held her before, that night she'd brought the tree and toy train.

Mmm...

Beneath Alex's sweatshirt his muscles were hard and she explored the contours of a man who'd worked not only with his mind, but his body. She didn't feel cold, though her thin shirt and jeans were hardly protection against the bitter chill that had descended over Puget Sound.

Pleasure shimmered in wave after wave as Alex began kissing his way down the curve of her neck. Then suddenly, a loud, raucous sound pierced the air.

"What?"

Alex jerked away, looking horrified, and Shannon dropped her hands to her side.

Think fast, she ordered her frozen brain, but it wasn't cooperating.

"Merrooooow."

Thank God.

She edged around Alex's stiff figure and looked for the source of distress. A kitten, all ears and eyes, stuck its head from under a bush and cried again.

"You poor thing," Shannon said, kneeling and holding out her hand. "Come here."

The kitten had obviously been fending for itself for a long time, because it hesitated, looking suspicious.

"It's all right, little one, I won't hurt you."

Alex stared at the ragged feline and wondered how it could resist that coaxing voice.

Damnation. How could he have kissed Shannon again?

He couldn't even blame her. She'd done everything but climb the wall trying to get away from him.

The cat put a hesitant foot on the flagstone patio, ready to bolt backward if the gentle voice turned out to have a mean hand attached to it.

"Come here, baby. No one is going to hurt you."

"Meooooow."

"Yes, I know. It's all right now." She cuddled the feline against her breasts and the air hissed from Alex's chest. He ached, but the physical pain was less intense than the torment in his mind.

Shannon O'Rourke had a filthy kitten tucked lovingly to her body, and he couldn't remember the last time he'd seen something so beautiful. Panic screamed through him, a warning of everything he didn't want to feel again.

"Shannon, we have to talk about what happened."

She glanced at him…and rolled her eyes. "For goodness sake, Alex, don't go melodramatic. I was upset and you gave me a friendly kiss. I'm surprised you didn't laugh your head off."

"About what?"

"What do you think? Remember the smoke alarm going off? Black smoke filling the air? I must have looked ridiculous."

The cookies.

Right.

His brain wasn't working correctly, but it was a relief to know Shannon hadn't taken him seriously. In fact, she'd been so upset, she probably hadn't noticed the more than friendly way he'd groped her body.

"I'm not being melodramatic, I was just wondering what you plan to do with that cat."

"Take it into your house, of course."

His eyes narrowed. "If you're thinking about giving it to Jeremy, the answer is no."

"I'm planning to adopt him myself. But I don't have a drop of milk in my house, so you're going to have to cough up the white stuff."

She strolled past him as if the last fifteen minutes had never occurred, and Alex shook his head. He'd missed something significant, but since he didn't have a clue what that significant something might be, he focused on a real problem.

"Wait, Shannon. Jeremy is going to see that cat and want it."

"You fuss too much. I'll explain everything to him," she said over her shoulder.

"Men don't 'fuss.'"

"Yeah, right."

She disappeared inside his house and he remained where he stood, amazed at the way the tables had been turned on him again. For a man who prided himself on being in control, he was losing it faster than a barrel sailing over Niagara Falls.

"Cats usually only clean themselves after they've eaten," Shannon told Jeremy as he sat in her arms, watching the tired kitten lick his oversize feet. "That's why he's so dirty. He hasn't eaten regularly for a while."

"Is he gonna be okay?"

"I think so. I'll take him to see my brother tomorrow. Connor is a cat doctor, and he'll make sure nothing is wrong."

"He looks scared."

"I know. He's been alone and trying to take care of himself for a while. I'm sure he wants to be loved, but it will take time for him to feel safe again."

Jeremy released a sigh and snuggled closer. "What's his name?"

She kissed his cheek; names seemed to be important to him. "Cats reveal their names when they're comfortable with you. He'll tell me when he's ready."

"*Shannon,* that's too fanciful," Alex warned.

She lifted her chin and gave him a narrow look.

Children needed a little fancy in their lives, and Jeremy had already seen too much reality. Besides, as far as she was concerned, Alex was skating on very thin ice. His relief at the way she'd dismissed their kiss had been practically insulting—particularly when she was certain that the kiss had shaken him as much as it had shaken her.

"You don't know much about cats," she retorted, "if you think that's fanciful."

"Oh?" He didn't say anything more, just crossed his arms over his chest and reminded her with his silence that he'd gone out in the rain and purchased the supplies she needed for a feline housemate.

Well, maybe the ice beneath his feet wasn't as thin as she'd thought.

The need to be fair did battle with her feminine pique, and fairness won. Alex *had* to be careful. He had Jeremy to think about, and she was never going to be nominated mother of the year.

The faint scent of smoke lingered in the house, and she wrinkled her nose. "I'm sorry about the cookies," she said to Jeremy. "I'm not very good at cooking."

He twisted and put his arms around her neck. "That's okay, Shannon. I don't care."

She blinked, still fighting those annoying tears. "I know a great bakery. They'd probably let us come and watch them bake a gingerbread house. We'll ask your daddy if it's all right."

"Can we go, Daddy?" Jeremy asked eagerly. "You can come, too."

It sounded like a careless afterthought and Shannon smothered a laugh. Yet she sobered quickly, remembering the pain Alex had expressed about Jeremy wanting to spend time with her rather than him. He worried about his son, like any good father. But while Jeremy was looking for a way out of the sadness, his daddy seemed determined to look backward, instead of reaching for the future.

Like the kitten, Alex probably wanted to be loved…he just didn't trust that it wouldn't end up hurting him.

She looked again at Alex's handsome features and the shadows that lingered in his eyes. He needed laughter. He needed to learn how to play and enjoy life.

He needed to stop being stuck in the past.

And so did she.

Chapter Eight

"Down you go, son," Alex said as Shannon opened the door of the bakery on Saturday. He lifted Jeremy from his shoulders and then held his hand as they stepped into the crisp outside air.

The scents of spice and vanilla and chocolate clung to their clothing and Shannon smiled.

It wasn't the New Year yet, but she'd made a resolution to look to the future, instead of being afraid of what it might *not* hold. Of course, that didn't mean she shouldn't be careful about Alex. He'd made it abundantly clear that he didn't want a permanent relationship with any woman, so falling for him wouldn't be smart.

In the meantime, it was almost like having a family of her own, the three of them walking down the holly- and pine-decorated street. She carried a box filled with perfect gingerbread people; they would add some to the Christmas tree when they got home, and others would be eaten with milk.

Naturally Alex hadn't let her pay for them. His stubborn pride was sweetly annoying, but she could forgive him. He hadn't teased her once about the burned cookies, or complained about the odor of smoke in his house.

"Ho, ho, ho," cried a sidewalk Santa, ringing his bell. "Merry Christmas."

Shannon reached into her purse and withdrew several bills and a handful of change to throw into his kettle.

"Why'd you do that, Shannon?" Jeremy asked

"Santa is trying to help people," she explained.

"Daddy doesn't believe in Santa."

She gave Alex a stern look. The man needed a kick in his scrumptious rear end.

He cleared his throat. "Actually, I said that Santa is more like a state of mind than someone real."

"Pop psychology rears its head again."

They stopped and Jeremy pressed his nose against a store window where mechanical figures simulated Santa's workshop. Santa wore striped stockings and glasses and peered intently at a half-finished fire engine.

"A little fantasy can't hurt," she said softly. "What's wrong with letting him believe?"

Alex pulled her farther from Jeremy's ears. "I can't do that, not after telling him everything would be all right when his mother got sick. It wasn't all right, and I knew it wouldn't be, but I still said it."

Shannon's heart skipped a beat. "Mom said it would be all right the day we buried my father."

"Then you know what I'm talking about. I've seen the way you miss your dad. What's all right about that?"

"You never stop missing the people you love," Shannon said, understanding better than ever before what her mother had tried to tell her. Life was a bittersweet tapestry, with sorrow and joy mixing into the pattern until they were nearly inseparable. "But Mom wasn't saying we'd forget Dad. She meant that we would go on and that there still would be good days. And there have been, even though he's gone...and the good is better because of who he was and what he left behind."

"Jeez, Shannon. How can you open yourself up like that?" Alex sounded almost angry. "You barely know us."

"I'm doing it because I don't want Jeremy to *be* like me, keeping it all inside. And I don't think his mother would want it, either."

Alex closed his eyes, shutting out the sight of Shannon's generous face, the gentle light in her eyes as she gazed at his son. Her breezy sophistication hid a tender side she had trouble revealing. But not when it came to Jeremy.

His chest ached, only he didn't know if it came from old sorrows, or the space Shannon was forcing him to make in his heart.

When they'd first met, her volatile nature had reminded him of his mother and father, but the comparison was fading. He found himself looking forward to each day, to their conversations and even to not knowing what to expect. There was a depth to Shannon that fascinated him...almost as much as it scared him.

Were there other choices? Other possibilities than the ones he'd chosen? Or would he just fall into the same angry hell that had destroyed his parents? He didn't believe he could ever break a marriage vow, but would he find himself stuck in the same screaming rounds of arguments and the bitter chill between those arguments?

Alex instinctively stepped backward, only to jump at the sudden blare of a car alarm.

"What the...?" He stared at the Jaguar parked at the curb. "I barely touched the damn thing."

Shannon shook her head. "I hate those things. They're so sensitive. I think just breathing sets them off."

"What happened, Daddy?" Jeremy's eyes were round and he clasped his fingers over his ears. "Make it stop."

Before Alex could answer, a man ran from a nearby jewelry shop and yelled. "What are you doing to my Jag?"

"Breathing," Alex shouted back.

Shannon burst out laughing, and he watched, loving the way she didn't care that they were attracting attention. It should have bothered him; he'd hated it when he was a kid and his parents fought in public places with everyone looking at them. But this was different.

The man bent over, anxiously checking the paint of his Jaguar, and Shannon impudently thumbed her nose at him.

Laughing now himself, Alex swung Jeremy into one arm, and put the other around Shannon.

"Is that any way for the O'Rourke Public Relations Director to act?" He thought for a moment. "For that matter, is it any way for an O'Rourke to act?"

"I'm on vacation."

She might be on vacation, but within minutes she had the Jag's owner eating from her hand, even getting him to admit he'd been in the wrong for yelling.

In downtown Seattle, the commotion would have hardly been noticed, but in their small community, it was an event. Christmas shoppers filled with seasonal goodwill paused and chatted. A policeman stopped and asked if he was needed. Assured he wasn't, he stayed nevertheless and ate the gingerbread cookie Shannon offered him.

Something that could have turned ugly became a social event, and it was all because of Shannon. She had a gift for bringing out the best in people—a sincere concern for others, a loving spirit that accepted human foibles and graces alike.

"We need more of these," she said when everyone had gone about their business. The box of cookies dangled from one finger, empty.

"Let's go back. They're yummy," Jeremy said, munching the cookie she'd given him first.

Alex thought about the excuses he ought to make, the things he had to do, the term papers and projects still to grade.

"I think we need more, too," he agreed. "And let's get some cocoa. I'm cold."

As they retraced their steps to the bakery, it occurred to him that he was getting too involved, but it was easy to push the worry to the back of his mind.

Because for the first time in longer than Alex could remember, he was happy.

Shannon hummed to herself as she read the new cookbook by the author of the not-so-foolproof ginger people recipe.

She'd always hated cookbooks—they seemed to be a reminder of something she couldn't do. But even if she couldn't cook to save her life, it was surprisingly interesting to see what was involved.

From the corner of her eye she saw the kitten, miraculously improved in appearance, sidle into the living room. He was at that awkward growing stage—all ears and brown tiger-stripe legs.

She knew if she was patient, he would eventually work his way up the couch and into her arms. It was the same every night. He'd watch from the doorway, resistant to coaxing, but by morning he purred beneath the comforter, curled against her tummy.

Would Alex be like that someday?

Cautious, guarding his heart, before finding himself in a woman's arms and loving her completely?

Shannon closed the cookbook and clung to her new-found peace. The restlessness that had worried her family and taken its toll on her staff was nearly gone, but that didn't mean she'd stopped wanting more from her life.

Her feelings for Alex had nothing to do with his proximity or the wonderful child he'd fathered, and they weren't because of her physical attraction to him, though heaven knew that was intense. Just kissing him was more exciting than anything she'd experienced with another man. But more than that, he was smart, hardworking and adored his son. He had a good sense of humor and a core of strength and integrity that was all too rare.

It would be so easy to love Alex, to give him the part of herself that no one had ever seen. She hadn't loved that boy in college; she realized that now. Not really. Not the way a woman loves a man. Her pride had been hurt, and she'd lost her girlish dreams, but there were other dreams.

A soft, warm body wriggled along her thigh, and she glanced down to see the kitten's anxious eyes.

So needy.

So ready to bolt.

So afraid to accept that his life had changed. To believe that food and kindness weren't a deception. That he could trust again.

Oh, Alex, she breathed silently. If there was ever someone who needed to be loved by a woman, it was him. But that woman wouldn't be her. He hadn't seemed to care about her culinary disaster, but he would eventually choose someone more like his first wife, if only for Jeremy's sake. That was what they both deserved, a real homemaker, and all the stolen kisses in the world wouldn't change that.

"I wish I could stay with you all day, little one," she whispered to the kitten. "But I can't."

He blinked and stretched out one paw, touching her arm.

A small overture that tugged at her heart.

At almost the same moment, sounds outside the front door made the feline's ears stand at attention. He darted into the kitchen when the bell rang.

It was the McKenzies. During their cookie outing the day before, they'd talked about having lunch together, though a time hadn't been discussed.

"Shannon?" Jeremy called. "Hurry."

"Coming." Shannon opened the door. "I take it you're hungry."

"More like cold." Alex shivered and stuck his hands in his pockets. "How can it feel colder here than in Minnesota?"

"It's the damp. You'll get used to it."

"If we stay."

The casual words made Shannon colder than the worst arctic storm. Swallowing, she stepped back to let them inside. "I didn't realize you were thinking about leaving."

He shrugged. "Just keeping my options open."

"Kitty, kitty," Jeremy called, looking hopefully around the room.

"He's still shy," Shannon said, trying to compose her expression. "You have to be patient." Excellent advice for herself, as well, except that men weren't cats, and they generally couldn't be won over with food and a warm place to sleep.

Alex wouldn't have had anything to do with her if it hadn't been for Jeremy. She needed to remind herself of that at frequent intervals.

"We called earlier, to see if you'd prefer having brunch, but you weren't here," he murmured, standing close to the embers of the small fire she'd built.

"I went to church."

"Oh."

His flat tone confirmed what Shannon had already guessed. She would have invited them to attend the service with her, but she figured Alex had turned his back on the church, along with so many other things.

"Um, I'll get my purse," she said quickly.

"There's no rush." He crouched by the hearth. "This feels good."

His jeans were stretched over his muscled legs and she held her breath, remembering how they'd felt, pressed against her.

Friends, she reminded herself.

Just friends.

She decided hurrying was a good idea, and she grabbed what she needed in record time. "I'm ready," she said, in case he hadn't noticed.

Standing, Alex closed the glass doors across the hearth— to prevent any sparks from the dying embers popping into the room while they were gone. His gaze went to the coat she wore, and she knew he'd expected to help her with it. The perfect gentleman. Just like her brothers, but it didn't make her knees weak to have *them* ease a coat up her arms.

"So…where do you want to eat?" he asked.

"Anywhere is fine."

Fine.

Inadvertently, Alex thought about the milk and cookies they'd eaten the evening before, made even better by laughter and talk. They'd discussed art and literature, history, travel and world affairs. Shannon was naturally curious and had asked perceptive questions about engineering and his work in less-developed countries, showing a healthy grasp of math and sciences.

His mind had shied away from thoughts that would only make him feel guilty, but the guilt was inevitable. Kim had been the dearest of women, and he'd loved her, but her interests had revolved around children and their home. Her priorities had made him comfortable; they hadn't always challenged his mind.

Shannon wasn't comfortable, he told himself firmly.

He still wanted comfortable. Things were comfortable the way they were, with just him and Jeremy.

Yeah? jeered Alex's conscience. So why are you spending so much time with Shannon?

The answer was something he didn't want to know.

"We're going, Jeremy. Where is Mr. Tibbles?" he asked.

Jeremy looked thoughtful, then he pointed to the rabbit, sitting by the Christmas tree. "Shannon says Mr. Tibbles might wanna stay home sometimes. He could stay here with kitty, and then he wouldn't be alone."

"That's a…a good idea." Startled, Alex looked from the rabbit to his son, and last to Shannon. She was watching Jeremy, nodding agreement, and he'd never felt so grateful in his life.

The hell with guilt, at least for today.

She'd performed a miracle and if they didn't have Jeremy as an audience, he'd give her another kiss. A friendly one, of course.

In fact…

"Shannon, may I see you in the other room for a moment?"

"Sure."

They walked into the kitchen, and Alex saw what he should have seen before: a room obviously not used for any serious cooking. He felt badly that he had asked her to do something she wasn't able to handle, though it had been endearing to see her so upset when she did everything *else* so well.

"Alex, is something—"

He smothered her question with his lips.

It was just a little, *friendly* kiss and he released her as fast as he'd grabbed her.

Shannon's green eyes were wide and startled. "Alex?"

"Thank you for Mr. Tibbles," he said, still exulting in the progress Jeremy had made.

"I…I didn't do anything."

"You did. I was right that first day—you have a gift with children. You're great with him."

He'd pleased her, he could tell by the way her cheeks bloomed pink. When was the last time Shannon had blushed? He'd bet it had been awhile.

"I'm going to warm up the Jeep," he said. "Be back in a few minutes."

Shannon touched her fingers to her mouth after Alex had disappeared. That kiss had been an impulse he'd probably regret, but she couldn't be sorry herself. His unstinting approval of her time with Jeremy filled an empty place in her soul.

Vacations weren't so bad, she thought.

Not if you could spend them doing something special.

A few days later, Shannon was even more convinced that vacations were a splendid invention. Instead of running her staff ragged with her favorite community projects for the past two and a half weeks, she was having fun. Going back to work would be a drag, but she'd survive. Besides, Kane was exceptionally generous with time off.

Shannon grinned.

If her brother had his druthers, the family would be living a life of perfect ease and luxury. He'd always wanted to give them far more than they wanted to take.

Still, as much fun as it was taking care of Jeremy, she *would* have to go back to work, and he'd have to go to daycare again. It might have been better if she and Alex had insisted he return once his cold was better, but they hadn't.

They?

Hmmm. *They* felt like a team, but Shannon wasn't good at deceiving herself. Alex was Jeremy's father; she was just the neighbor.

Torrents of rain splattered the window and Shannon frowned, uneasiness replacing her contentment. The rain had begun Sunday night and hadn't stopped since. The ground was already saturated with water and flooding was predicted in the lowland areas and along the White River.

It was silly, yet the feeling that something was wrong grew over the next hour. She checked on Jeremy several times, but nothing was amiss.

Was it Alex?

She wished he was safely home, but he was in the middle of giving his last exam, with the afternoon session yet to come. Anyway, he was driving the Jeep, and it was designed for rugged driving. She recalled some of the stories he'd told her about building dams and roads in parts of the world where rain and mud were a daily part of life. The simple stories had revealed a man who worked hard and well; Alex could handle anything Mother Nature threw at him.

But she still felt uneasy. She often got those sensations at work, the prickling at the back of her neck when something wasn't quite right. The public relations staff claimed it made them nervous the way her instincts worked, but they'd learned to pay attention.

Shannon finally dialed her deputy, waiting impatiently while the phone rang several times.

"O'Rourke Enterprises." Chris's normally measured tone sounded slightly frantic.

"Chris, it's Shannon."

"Where have you been?" he demanded. "I've been calling and calling."

She winced, realizing she'd left her cell phone at her condo. "I'm at a friend's house. What's wrong?"

"The factory near Bolton is flooding and we have two employees missing. Please come, Shannon. I don't want to be the one to tell their wives."

She closed her eyes and said a silent prayer for the missing men. "I'll be there as soon as possible. Do you know if any of the roads between here and Seattle are closed?"

"No. I checked with the roads department in case you were already on the way and had got stuck."

"All right. I'm babysitting a friend's little boy, so I'll have to bring him with me. Have someone meet us in the garage and make sure they understand Jeremy isn't to be left alone for a minute. Tell them if he gets scared about anything, they'll answer to me."

She issued several additional orders then put the phone down, thinking carefully. She'd dealt with numerous crises since becoming her brother's public relations director, but she'd never had a child to worry about at the same time. No matter what else happened, Jeremy mustn't get frightened.

"Jeremy?" she said, going into the den where he was watching a Christmas video.

He gave her an angelic smile.

"I hope you don't mind, but I have something to do at my office. We need to drive into Seattle." Luckily, Alex had insisted they put a spare booster seat in her Mercedes in case it was needed.

"Can we have pizza?" he asked hopefully.

Pizza seemed to be the magic cure-all, and despite her concern for the missing employees, Shannon smiled. "Sure, we can have pizza. Go get your coat."

Jeremy sang "Jingle Bells" all the way, and by the time she pulled into her reserved parking spot by the executive elevator, she was certain that "Jingle Bells" had been written by a sadist.

Three members of her staff were waiting, including her deputy, and he rushed over with a relieved smile on his face. "It's all right," he whispered the minute the driver's door opened. "The men have been found. Only minor injuries."

Most of Shannon's tension vanished.

That was all that mattered. Damage to property could be repaired—it wasn't the first time it had happened, and it wouldn't be the last. Damage to lives couldn't always be fixed.

"Great. Everyone, this is Jeremy," she said, lifting him in her arms. "He's a special friend of mine, and he loves pizza. So we need to order a whole bunch."

Chapter Nine

Alex turned into the underground parking garage of O'Rourke Enterprises and stopped at the security gate.

A uniformed guard stepped from the kiosk. "Can I help you, sir?"

"My name is Alex McKenzie. My son is—"

"Yes, Dr. McKenzie, we've been expecting you," the man said quickly. "Ms. O'Rourke said you wouldn't want to be delayed. Follow the white arrows to the center of this level. A parking space is available by the elevator."

"Thank you." Alex pulled forward, eyebrows raised. Shannon appeared to have thought of everything.

He'd been thrown by her phone message saying she'd brought Jeremy into the office. He trusted her, but he knew how hard it was for his son to adjust to new people.

The elevator doors opened as Alex got out of the Jeep, and a woman in a business suit hurried over.

"Hello, Dr. McKenzie. I'm Claire Hollings, Ms.

O'Rourke's executive assistant. Welcome to O'Rourke Enterprises. Jeremy is doing fine," she said before Alex could ask.

He smiled faintly. Shannon had her staff well-trained. He was impressed. "Thank you."

"Come with me, sir."

When the elevator doors closed, Alex rolled his shoulders to release his lingering tension. Shannon's brief message had only said there had been an incident at one of the O'Rourke companies, and that she'd needed to take Jeremy to the office with her.

"If you don't mind my asking, what happened?" he asked.

Claire Hollings inserted an override key into the control panel and pushed the button to one of the top floors. "Flooding at our textile factory in Bolton. Our emergency response team is on the scene."

"I hope no one is hurt."

Claire flashed a bright smile, which melted her brisk demeanor. "Minor injuries, that's all. Two men were missing, but they've been found and they're fine except for one broken arm and some cuts and bruises."

The elevator rapidly ascended and opened to a spacious office suite.

"This way," Claire said, gesturing with her hand.

They threaded their way through a beehive of activity. He overheard references to Shannon, what she'd told them to do, wondering what would she think, relief that she'd come. Their destination was a glass-walled office in the very back and Alex saw his son sitting behind the desk, looking intently at a laptop computer. The woman with him said something and he looked up, waved madly, then focused on the computer again.

It was disconcerting.

Until recently, Alex had been the focus of his son's life, the linchpin in a world that had lost its balance. But things were changing now that Shannon's outgoing nature was rubbing off on Jeremy.

"Ms. O'Rourke is in the middle of a press conference," Claire explained, pointing to a bank of televisions.

Shannon was speaking on the muted sets, her name and title emblazoned at the bottom of the screen, where microphones featuring various television station logos could be seen.

"Would you like to listen?" asked her assistant.

Intrigued, Alex nodded, and Claire increased the volume.

"...just grateful the injuries weren't more severe."

"What about the employees' jobs, Shannon?" called a reporter from offscreen. "How long before the mill is up and running again? Christmas is a tough time to go without a paycheck."

"No jobs will be lost, and there won't be any loss of wages," she answered. "But it will be several weeks before production begins again."

"We've heard a number of homes were damaged, as well. Do some of them belong to your workers?" asked someone else.

"That's correct. We have emergency response teams assessing the needs of each family, and assistance will be offered as needed. But let me emphasize that our services are available to everyone. Bolton is a fine community and we want to help wherever it's needed."

"Are any relief agencies on the scene?"

"Yes, shelters are being set up..." She continued, explaining the locations and aid available. Alex leaned against a desk and watched, fascinated by the play of emotions on her face. Efficient, reassuring…compassion for the injured and distressed. Anyone watching would soon be convinced the world would right itself.

The way she'd been making Alex believe. The kernels of hope Shannon had managed to plant were taking root.

"She's good, isn't she?"

Alex tore his attention from the television. A man stood nearby, and though his hair and eyes were dark, there wasn't any question this was one of Shannon's brothers.

"She's great."

"Kane O'Rourke," the man said, putting out his hand.

"Alex McKenzie."

"So I'm told. Shannon says you're an engineer. If you're interested, I may have a consulting job for you on that factory."

Alex frowned. "You don't know whether I'm qualified."

"Don't worry, I'll check your credentials," Kane said dryly. "But I know my sister, and she thinks you're the man for the job."

"They called, Mr. O'Rourke. Your helicopter is ready," interrupted Claire Hollings.

"Thank you, Claire."

Kane turned back to Alex.

"Glad to meet you, McKenzie. I'm flying over to see my injured employees, but I'll be in touch."

Alex shook his head as Shannon's brother strode away. Consulting for O'Rourke Enterprises would look good on his résumé, but he wasn't sure how he felt about his life becoming even more entangled with those of the O'Rourkes.

He went into Shannon's office and ruffled his son's hair.

"I appreciate you staying with him," he told the woman sitting with Jeremy.

"It was a pleasure. Your son has a strong aptitude for computers," she added. "I hope to see you again, Jeremy."

"Bye, Bobbi. We don't haf to leave yet, do we, Daddy?"

"Yes, we do."

But he'd barely gotten Jeremy's coat fastened before Shannon appeared, surrounded by people clamoring for her attention. She gave him an apologetic smile. "I'm so sorry about bringing Jeremy into Seattle," she said when the tumult had settled. "But things were frantic here."

"Don't worry about it," Alex assured. "It probably was good for him."

It was true, yet the truth bothered him, because it led to questions without answers. *Would* Jeremy have had an easier adjustment the past year if his mother had encouraged him to be more independent? Kim had spent every waking moment with their son and had wanted him to be educated at home. Was that why Jeremy was desperately unhappy in day-care? Would he hate school even more?

A weary sigh escaped his throat, and Alex felt the inevitable stab of guilt. Kim wasn't here to defend her decisions—decisions she'd had to make alone because *he'd* been off building roads and bridges in remote corners of the world.

"I'll get Jeremy out of here, so you can work," he said. "And I'm the one who should apologize. You've done more than anyone has a right to expect. It must have been inconvenient with everything you had to do."

Emotions he couldn't read shifted in Shannon's eyes. "It wasn't inconvenient. He ate pizza and played on the computer."

"Well, thanks, anyway."

Jeremy gave her a hug, dragging his feet and making it plain he wanted to stay. Alex knew how he felt, and he turned around at the door.

"How long will you have to stay in the city?"

"I don't know. A few more hours. But I shouldn't have to come in tomorrow, so I can still sit with Jeremy."

She would be tired when she got home. Alex had dealt with emergencies when he was working in the field, and knew what it was like once the pressure and adrenaline wore off.

"I…" He cleared his throat. Stepping along the edge of a precipice was never easy, and that was what it was like around Shannon. But surely he could be a good enough friend to do something for *her* this time. "If you want to talk later, I'll be up."

Surprise flickered across her face. "All right."

He hustled Jeremy away, aware that curious glances were being sent in their direction. The O'Rourke employees were wondering who he was, and what he meant to Shannon. It wouldn't have been so bad if he could tell them, but he couldn't.

It was another one of those damned questions without an answer.

Stomach churning from her encounter with Alex, Shannon sank in her chair. He hadn't seemed upset about her bringing Jeremy into the city, yet who could tell?

"Nice kid," Claire said, sticking her head inside the office. "And nice man. I haven't seen a body like that since I went to Montana last summer."

She gave her assistant a dismissive look. "He's a widower, Claire. We're just friends."

"What? Widowers don't need sex?"

Needing sex wasn't the problem. Shannon had seen and felt the intensity of Alex's response to her, a response he didn't welcome. He insisted it had nothing to do with her, but it still hurt.

Shannon pasted a practiced smile on her lips and waved her hand. "Go back to work," she ordered. "I have things to do, even if you don't."

"Hah. I always have work. My boss is a slave driver."

"Slave driver? I thought I was the dragon lady."

"Knew we'd get a rise out of you over that one."

"And I knew you were the one to come up with it. So scat."

Claire grinned and returned to her desk, while Shannon pulled up damage reports on her computer. Things were settling down. Kane would visit the various emergency shelters and decide if more needed to be done, but his response teams were well-trained. She was lucky to work for a company with near-limitless resources, and a CEO willing to use them.

Shannon sighed. It had almost been a relief to handle something familiar. Spending time with Jeremy was easy; figuring Alex out wasn't.

Alex.

She spun her chair around and gazed out at the city. Rain continued to pour and she knew there'd be more flooding, more problems. It was inevitable. Mother Nature was stronger than the best-laid plans.

Like her plan to help Jeremy.

Dear heaven. Her eyes closed. Where was her common sense? She was running headlong toward another heartbreak, seduced by a sweet little boy and a man who made her feel more than she'd believed possible.

But she couldn't help herself.

* * *

Five hours later, Shannon was grateful she'd promised Kane not to drive herself home. The company driver detoured to avoid one flooded street after another, but peace reigned inside the limousine. The trappings of wealth weren't important to her, but they could be convenient.

She was drowsing when the door opened and the chauffeur extended his hand. "Miss O'Rourke, we're here."

"Thanks, Ted." She slid from the limo and looked to see if the lights were on in Alex's condo. The downstairs windows were still lit; Jeremy would be in bed, but his daddy seemed to be awake.

"I'll just walk you to the door," Ted insisted when she tried to take the umbrella he held over her head. "And check the house for any problems."

"You need to get home, Ted."

"I have my orders, ma'am."

"I'll take care of Miss O'Rourke," said Alex as he walked down the driveway.

"Sheesh. Doesn't anybody think I can take care of myself?" Shannon demanded.

The two men looked at her blankly. They didn't get it, but neither did any of her brothers. Ted's orders might have come from Kane, but the driver was the father of three grown daughters and would have walked her to the door without being told. He was the old-fashioned type, just like Alex.

She sighed. Her independence wasn't being challenged. They were just big, dumb brutes who couldn't help themselves.

"Never mind. Thank you, Ted, for driving me home. I'll be all right with Alex. He's a friend."

Ted examined Alex the way a cop would examine a suspect in a police lineup. "Very well. I've arranged for your car to be delivered in the morning."

Shannon chuckled as the limo rolled smoothly away.

"I'm glad you think it's funny," Alex muttered, pulling her into his house. "Half of the state is flooded. How do you handle this much rain?"

"We tread water." Shannon dropped onto the couch. "I suppose Jeremy is in bed already."

"An hour ago. Have you had anything to eat?"

She thought about it. "Cold pizza around six. We were going to order food, but most of the restaurants aren't delivering because of the weather."

Alex let out a disgusted sound. "I'll get you something."

"No, I'm fine."

She might as well have been talking to a rock. He tossed the umbrella into a corner and headed for the kitchen.

Shannon hauled herself to her feet and followed. "Do you ever listen?"

"It's one of my failings. Deal with it."

He was so endearingly rumpled and belligerent that she laughed again.

Alex gazed at Shannon, her face less weary now that she was laughing, and realized he must have done something right. Who could have guessed that being grumpy and out-of-sorts would do anything but start an argument? In his family it would have triggered World War Three.

She was amazing, and while he wanted to tell her that, the words stuck in his throat.

"Do you like omelets?" he asked instead.

"Yes. You cook omelets?"

"Sure, they're..." Alex stopped. He'd almost said they

were easy, but cooking was a touchy subject for Shannon. "I manage."

He pulled eggs from the refrigerator, then nearly dropped them when she yawned and stretched, her body arching like a sensuous cat.

Friends, he reminded himself.

With a sleepy smile she drifted into the utility room and he heard the dryer being opened and closed. Sounds of daily tasks that were never quite done.

"Come out of there, you're supposed to be relaxing," he called.

"In a min—oh, *damn*."

Alex had never heard Shannon curse and he hurried to see what had happened. The smell of bleach hit him instantly, and he saw that she'd somehow upended the bottle in a basket. A basket full of his jeans.

It struck him as inordinately funny, but he didn't think she'd agree. He dumped the contents of the basket into the washing machine and hoped for the best, though he had a feeling the jeans were beyond rescue. He hoped Shannon's pride wasn't in the same condition.

He cast a cautious glance in her direction.

She'd backed against the wall, her face stormy with frustration.

There was only one thing Alex could think of doing. He put an arm around her waist and used his free hand to cup her chin so she'd have to look at him. "If you think I give a hoot about what happens to those jeans when you can make my son smile, then you're crazy."

"I'm a real riot."

"Treasure is more like it," he retorted. "I can pay people to clean and cook. What you do for Jeremy is priceless."

"You sound like a credit-card commercial," Shannon grumbled, but he could see a smile overtaking her scowl.

"Not a chance." Alex dropped a kiss on her nose. "Did you know that in some cultures the smell of bleach is an aphrodisiac?"

"You're making that up."

He wasn't so sure. In the right circumstances bleach probably could excite a man. *Like now.* Like when a beautiful, sensual woman crowded everything else from his mind.

This time his kiss landed on her mouth and lingered for an endless moment.

Definitely an aphrodisiac.

"Um…mmphf…Alex?" Shannon said. "What about our agreement?"

"It's just a friendly kiss."

"Oh. Okay."

He gave her another, deeper and friendlier than ever, his tongue thrusting into the warm recesses of her mouth. She had textures a man could spend forever exploring, from the top of her fiery head to the bottom of those determined feet.

Like her hips.

They were slim and curved in the right place. Blood gathered, hot and heavy at the top of his thighs, and he pressed his forehead to Shannon's in a desperate attempt to regain control.

Yeah, friendly.

So friendly that in another minute he would have invited her to share his king-size bed for the night.

Their breaths intermingled and he swallowed. A month ago, he would have believed the need in him was because he missed Kim so much. But Shannon wasn't a substitute for anyone; she'd created a whole new kind of needing.

"I better get that omelet going," he said hoarsely.

Or you'll be eating it for breakfast.

The unspoken words hung in the air, and he knew Shannon had heard them in the silence. But he couldn't be the man she deserved. He was too damaged, grieving his first love, unwilling to take a chance that his life wouldn't turn into the turmoil he remembered from his parents' marriage.

Yet he knew if he had met Shannon in a different space and time, he would have held on to her like a child grabbing the shiniest star in the sky.

"I'll go now," he whispered and she nodded.

Eggs had never been beaten with more vigor than the ones Alex broke into the bowl, or cheese more fiercely grated and peppers chopped. His preference would have been to lift weights or go running to release the energy twisting his nerves, but neither was an option.

"My salsa is the atomic-heat variety," he said, plunking the plate in front of Shannon. "But you're welcome to it."

"I like spicy, remember?"

Alex pulled the jar from the fridge and put it next to her plate. He liked the way she wasn't cautious, the way she spooned the salsa generously over her eggs and ate, sighing with pleasure at the simple fare.

He liked being around her, even enjoyed her unpredictability, and that was new for him, as well.

"I must have been hungry, after all," Shannon said when she'd taken the last bite of omelet.

"Cold pizza isn't very satisfying."

"I know, but I'm not allowed to use the microwave in the employee break room."

Alex managed to keep a straight face, but it was a struggle. He could well imagine what had led to her being banned from using the microwave. And Shannon, being Shannon, wouldn't ask someone else to do it for her. "That's too bad. How about going into the living room and putting your feet up?" Changing the subject seemed prudent.

"I should go home. The cat will think he's been abandoned."

"Relax for a while. I'll go get No-Name so you can reassure him."

"No-Name?" she repeated.

"That's right. I'm assuming he hasn't 'revealed' his name to you yet. I have to call him something, so No-Name fits."

"You're a riot," Shannon said, but she let herself be convinced. She wanted to stay. Her condo might be beautifully furnished and decorated, but she felt more comfortable in Alex's home than in her own.

She was half asleep when Alex returned, dropping the kitten on her tummy. The feline let out a cry that sounded more annoyed than mournful, and cocked his head to one side.

Alex grinned. "He didn't like you being gone."

"He's been getting friendlier. It's hard learning to trust again," she murmured idly, extending a finger to the cat.

The kitten was already gaining weight, the bony ridges on his back no longer so prominent. In a few months he'd be a magnificent long-haired tabby, filled with the arrogance of his species. She didn't know why she hadn't gotten a cat years ago. They were amazing creatures, filled with secrets and purring wiles.

Alex sat at the end of the couch, pulled her feet into his lap and began massaging them.

Mmm. She'd never had a foot rub before, and it made her tense muscles turn to warm honey. How had he known exactly what she needed, when she didn't know herself?

"Alex?" she murmured.

"Yes?"

"Um…never mind." She wanted to ask why he had kissed her, but didn't want to spoil the moment. If she asked, he might stop rubbing her feet, and that would be a shame.

Yet the thought lingered, adding to the slide of heat in her veins.

Alex hadn't wanted her to be upset or hurt, and instead of getting annoyed that she'd spilled bleach on his clothing, he'd kissed her. Men had romanced her with flowers and jewelry and expensive restaurants over the years, but none of them had come close to Alex McKenzie and his simple omelet.

The Christmas-tree lights winked and twinkled, Alex's thumbs moved in slow, easy circles, and the kitten purred on her tummy.

She smiled and closed her eyes.

For the first time in forever, she was right where she wanted to be.

Chapter Ten

The phone on Alex's bedside table rang. He opened bleary eyes and looked at the clock.

Six?

What maniac would call at six in the morning?

"Yeah," he mumbled into the receiver.

"Where in hell is my sister, McKenzie? She isn't answering her phone."

Alex rubbed his face and yawned. The voice sounded like Kane O'Rourke's, and his tone was a far cry from their cordial encounter of the previous day. So much for a consulting job with O'Rourke Enterprises.

"She's here."

A harsh breath came over the line, followed by a woman's muffled voice, saying that Shannon was an adult, entitled to her own life. And would Kane please not interfere.

Good advice.

Alex yawned again. "Shannon fell asleep on the couch. She'd had a rough day and I didn't feel like kicking her out."

"I...see."

"Is this just a social call or is it something important?"

A brief silence was followed by a laugh. "Not important. I just wanted to talk to my sister." The woman whispered again in the background. "And my wife says to apologize for waking you up."

"Would you apologize if I'd said Shannon was in bed with me?"

"Probably not."

At least they understood each other.

"Okay. Wait while I see if she's awake." Leaving the phone on the table, Alex wandered downstairs. Shannon lay on the couch and he tried not to see how she made the room seem alive, though her eyes were closed.

He drifted back upstairs. "Sorry, O'Rourke. Out like a light," he told Kane. "I'll let her know you called."

He crawled back into bed, but sleep proved elusive. While Kane O'Rourke had been out of line, his love and concern for his sister was undeniable. Alex wasn't even sure he had Gail's current phone number, and the last time he'd seen her was at Kim's wake. They hadn't really talked, but not talking was a McKenzie trademark.

Mentally calculating the time difference between Washington and Japan, Alex reached for his address book. But when the ringing began, second thoughts had him ready to disconnect.

The Japanese greeting on the other end of the line momentarily threw him, then he said, "Gail?"

"Yes, this is Gail McKenzie."

Cripes, she didn't even recognize his voice. "It's Alex."

Silence, likely from shock. "Alex? Hi."

He swore to himself. This was even harder than he'd imagined. "How have you been, Gail?"

"Busy. You know how it is."

Did he ever.

"Yeah, I'm busy, too."

They exchanged painful small talk for five minutes before Gail excused herself. Alex was never more grateful to end a call, and he swiped beads of sweat from his forehead. Why had he bothered?

Shannon, he thought. He'd bothered because of Shannon. Beneath her polished veneer was a woman with old-fashioned family values, who prodded his conscience without even trying.

Like a ghost creeping through the house, Jeremy walked past Alex's bedroom door, dragging his blanket behind him. He spent a lot of time in front of the Christmas tree, probably dreaming of Shannon becoming his new mommy. Alex groaned, knowing his son would find the object of his dreams on the couch. Still, it wouldn't help to rush down and explain things Jeremy wouldn't believe anyway.

A delighted "Shannon" drifted up the stairs, his son's voice filled with the breathless excitement most children reserved for Disneyland and Santa Claus.

"A man ought to be able to sleep in his own house," Alex grumbled. But when the house was quiet again, he found sleep was the last thing on his mind. It was too full of visions of Shannon, the frustration in her eyes turning to laughter. Of her breathless anticipation before a kiss. Of Shannon holding his son, reading or just talking to him.

Why should *that* be so haunting? he wondered.

Over the past months he'd seen too many women trying to mother his son, their gushy concern spilling over to him. He moved across the country to get away from it.

"Damnation." Alex kicked the blankets away. He preferred sleeping in the nude, but with Shannon spending the night on the couch, he'd opted for pajamas. *That* was why he couldn't sleep. Those damned pj's.

Yeah, right.

A grim smile twisted Alex's lips as he got dressed. He was lousy at lying to himself.

Shannon read a story to Jeremy, her senses tuned to Alex's movements on the second floor. She hadn't slept so well in months, though it *had* been a surprise to wake up on her neighbor's couch with Jeremy standing over her. She must have fallen asleep after Alex's wonderful foot massage.

A smile curved her mouth.

Alex would probably never know how much his touch had stimulated other parts of her body. But it was his gentleness that had truly melted her.

Footfalls on the staircase had Shannon looking up. "Good morning."

"Morning." Alex yawned. "Your brother called. He's prepared to beat me senseless for letting you spend the night."

"He is not."

"Yes, he is. He tried calling you at home, then decided you might be here. I don't know why. Maybe he interrogated the chauffeur or something."

Shannon wanted to crawl under the couch. "Honestly, I told him we were just friends."

"Uh-huh."

"He means well."

"His wife told him you were an adult and not to interfere. She also told him to apologize." Alex grinned. "Do you want to go out for breakfast? I have a meeting with some folks at the university, but not until ten."

"I'd like that." She breathed a sigh of relief. At least he thought Kane's reaction was funny. "Do I have time to shower and change? It won't take long."

"Go ahead. I need to get Jeremy dressed, anyway."

Shannon carried the kitten home and got ready in record time. The phone rang before she could leave, and she picked it up, knowing it would be her oldest brother.

"Hey, sis."

She scowled. "Don't hey me. How could you call Alex like that? It's none of your business whether or not I'm sleeping with him. Besides, I told you we were just friends."

"I overreacted."

"As usual." She looked at her watch. "But we'll discuss it later. Do you have a reason for calling? I'm on vacation."

Kane chuckled, kindly refraining from reminding her that he'd forced her to take that vacation. "Nothing that can't keep. Talk to you later, sis."

Shannon said good-bye and hurried outside. It was still raining, and Alex got out of the Jeep to help her into the front seat. He looked wider awake than she'd ever seen him look in the morning, and his smile was brighter than sunshine.

"Thank you," he whispered.

"For getting ready so fast?"

"Better than that." He went around to the driver's seat and got in. "Jeremy, why don't you tell Shannon what you've just told me."

She twisted in her seat to look at the four year old. "Yes?"

"I'm not playing wolf an'more, 'cause Daddy has to work." He sighed a very adult sigh. "An' I guess I haf to go to day-care. After Christmas," he added hastily.

Pleasure went through Shannon. She'd wondered if she was doing the right thing, talking to Jeremy about his pretending to be sick and needing to accept day-care. She'd also planned to tell Alex about those talks, but there had never seemed to be a right time.

"You're a good boy. I'm so proud of you."

Jeremy glowed.

And Alex...the warmth in his eyes was the best reward she'd ever received. But it didn't mean anything had changed between them. He'd told her often enough he wasn't interested in a permanent relationship.

They drove to a local café. As they walked inside, Alex put his hand on the small of her back, sending shivers in all directions. "That okay?" he asked, pointing to a booth by the window.

"It's fine." He could have suggested a bench in the middle of a rain puddle and it would have been fine. She had it bad, and there wasn't a single reason to hope things were going to change. Yet a bubble of hope kept rising, demanding attention.

"I've been thinking," Shannon said once the waitress had taken their orders. "If Kane didn't annoy you too much, would you and Jeremy like to spend Christmas day with my family?"

A dark expression flickered in Alex's eyes, his barriers popping up one by one. "I don't know..."

"Oooh. Can we, Daddy?" Jeremy begged.

Alex hesitated, torn.

His first impulse was to refuse, but it *was* a chance for his son to see a real family celebration. On the other hand, Jeremy already had too many dreams about Shannon. It was Alex's fault. There was something he hadn't anticipated in his agreement to be just friends…Shannon was too irresistible.

To both of them.

"I'm sorry," she said worriedly. "I should have asked when we were alone. I understand if you have other plans."

He couldn't handle her apologizing. Not when she'd done so much for both of them.

"Actually, we don't have plans. We accept."

"Does that mean yes, Daddy?"

He nodded and Jeremy wriggled with excited anticipation. "Goody!"

"What should we bring?" Alex asked, already regretting the decision. He didn't know how to act with big families. His own was a mess, and Kim's only relatives had been distant cousins. Was there a particular protocol that was expected?

"Just bring yourselves. I have twin nieces who are close to Jeremy's age. They'll love playing with him."

The nieces sounded good; Jeremy needed to learn how to play with children his age. The day-care center had said he stayed too much to himself. Of course, Kane O'Rourke would be more convinced than ever that his little sister was involved with someone he didn't know anything about, but Alex took a perverse pleasure in the knowledge. If he ever *did* take Shannon to bed, he didn't plan on answering to anyone about it.

What about Kim?

It wasn't a new thought, and he knew it was something he'd have to deal with sooner or later. Strangely, he wanted to talk with Shannon about feeling guilty. Would she understand?

"We still should bring something," he said gruffly.

Shannon nodded. "You can bring me. I always have a mountain of stuff to take, and your Jeep would be perfect to pile it into."

"Then it's at your service."

"Good. We'll go Christmas morning and spend the day, if that's okay with you. Someone could drive me home if you decide we're too much for you."

"Mmm," he said noncommittally.

Their meal came and they talked about the weather and other safe subjects, and Shannon couldn't help being discouraged again. Alex had places inside she couldn't reach.

"You didn't eat much," Alex said when she pushed her plate away.

"I'm still full of omelet."

His eyes asked silently if something was wrong and she bit her lip. She doubted he was aware of the way he posted barriers and stay-out messages.

"It's after eight-thirty," she said, gesturing to the clock on the café wall. "You don't want to be late."

He agreed and took care of the bill.

It was funny, Shannon thought as they walked out to the Jeep. The more they seemed like a family, the more it hurt to know they were just playing a game.

Later in the morning, Shannon summoned her courage and opened Alex's washing machine. At home she managed basic care of underclothes and such, but the cleaning service took care of the big stuff. She knew what bleach could do to clothing, though, and she held her breath as she pulled Alex's jeans from the machine.

"Drat," she muttered, looking at the faded blotches. The two well-worn pairs didn't look so bad; they'd already lost a lot of color. But the newer ones were a mess.

The intimacy of doing a man's laundry had never struck her before, but now she was acutely aware of how those jeans wrapped around Alex's hips and muscled thighs. Maybe that was why some women liked doing laundry; it made them feel closer to their men.

She hastily shoved the jeans into the dryer and set it to low, the way the labels suggested.

"I am losing my mind," she said, glaring at the machine that thumped and thudded as the heavy jeans tumbled around inside. "Positively bonkers. Laundry is just work, not a mission in life. And I'm terrible at it."

Besides, it was too disturbing spending time in the utility room. All she could think about was Alex's kisses, the mix of tenderness and laughter. He'd been so kind about her fumble with the bleach bottle, though it must have been annoying.

She went into the kitchen and picked up the phone. She didn't have to be good at domestic skills if she knew who to call. The service who cleaned her condo could do an emergency job on Alex's house, instead of her taking the chance of ruining something else.

He'd probably be relieved.

As Alex parked in the drive late in the afternoon, he saw a car pulling out of Shannon's. Despite the rain he was able to make out two women inside, and they were waving at him.

"Can I help you?" he asked when the driver stopped and rolled down her window.

"No, we're from the cleaning service," the woman explained. "You must be Dr. McKenzie. Sorry about your jeans," she added with a grin.

Alex realized they must have talked to Shannon. She would have hated admitting what had happened. "It was an accident."

"Obviously. Gotta go."

He frowned as he opened his front door and the scent of lemon and baking surrounded him. They were fragrances from the past, a time when he'd arrived to a house freshly cleaned and a cobbler cooling on the stove. After being raised as an unwanted foster child, Kim had been determined to do things right. Maybe that was why she'd kept Jeremy close at home and insisted he eat a certain way.

"What is going on, Shannon?" he asked the minute he saw her on the couch wrapping gifts.

"Nothing. Jeremy is taking a nap and I had the cleaning service come," she said, looking up from the package she was taping. "They baked an apple cake, too. I figured you wouldn't want me to destroy anything else."

She'd assumed her polished veneer, the one that hid everything, and he sighed.

"I told you that stuff doesn't matter."

Her eyelashes swept down and she carefully measured a length of silver Christmas ribbon. "It matters to most men."

Maybe. Once upon a time he'd even been that kind of man. Hell, he'd *enjoyed* the way Kim catered to his every whim. Unfortunately, it had also let him off the hook to be a real father and husband. He ought to have insisted Jeremy be allowed to play with other children and have occasional treats like pizza, but he'd chosen the easy route.

It was sobering to realize that in his efforts not to repeat the mistakes of his parents, screaming and yelling and never agreeing, he'd made a different mistake. Parenting ought to be something a mother and father did *together,* balancing each other's strengths and weaknesses.

Shannon tied the ribbon around the package and he sighed again. Someone had hurt her in the past; probably someone a lot like him.

"Who told you men were like that?"

"I didn't have to be told."

"We both know there's more to it," he said, sitting and taking the spool of ribbon from her fingers. "Talk to me."

"Hey, if we're trading failed romance stories, you have to go first." She made it sound like a joke, and breath hissed through his teeth. *Damned stubborn woman.*

"There isn't much to tell, except for the way I left my wife and child eight months out of the year to pursue work I could have done at home. Does that qualify?"

"Alex. That isn't…that's not what I meant."

"I know." His tone gentled and he traced the line of her jaw. "But I don't know how to make you believe me."

She wrinkled her nose. "For heaven's sake, it's no big deal. It's just that your wife was a gifted homemaker, and I obviously come up short compared to her. Even success-ful career women have episodes of insecurity, you know."

"You could never come up short," Alex said, appalled. "You made my son come alive again."

You made me *come alive again.*

He now understood at a gut level why his parents had got-ten married despite their gross incompatibility—they'd felt more alive together than apart. To be really alive, you had to feel deeply, and Alex had done his best to wall himself away from emotion. Shannon tried to hide her deepest emotions, but they were an integral part of her heart and soul.

What would it be like being the man she felt safe enough to turn to when she was vulnerable and upset, instead of trying to be strong for everyone else?

Alex swallowed.

He wasn't that man.

Was he?

"Listen to me. I don't give a hoot about the cooking or cleaning," he insisted. "It was never about housekeeping when I said I wasn't…well…"

"Getting married again?" she finished for him.

"Yes. The truth is, I wasn't a great husband," he admitted. It was a relief to say it out loud, maybe because he knew Shannon wouldn't judge him.

Shannon shook her head. "I saw Kim's pictures. I know you made her happy. Isn't that the real measure of a husband?"

He hoped that was true.

Alex had never been a cuddler, but he had a sudden need to do just that. He gave Shannon a sideways glance, wondering how she'd feel about it.

"Do you have to leave right away?" he asked.

"No. Do you need to go out again?"

He shook his head. "Just checking." Getting up, he turned off the lights except those on the Christmas tree, then he sat on the floor and pulled Shannon down with him.

"Alex?"

His "just being friendly" routine from the night before stuck in his throat, so he settled her against his chest and inhaled the fragrance that clung to her hair and skin. He was still concerned about Jeremy and spending Christmas with Shannon's family, but he needed a moment of peace. The curious part was seeking peace with a woman who'd turned his routine and self-control on its ear.

"Aren't you worried about Jeremy finding us like this?" Shannon asked after a while.

"I worry about everything. It's one of my defining characteristics."

He sensed, more than heard, her laugh.

"Then why are we still sitting here?"

"I don't know, but it feels good. Tell me more about No-Name," he whispered, wanting to prolong the stolen interlude.

"His *name* is Magellan, for the explorer, because he has a tendency to find unusual routes through things. But there isn't much to tell. He's skittish and distrustful and hates loud noises, and he's so anxious to be loved that it breaks my heart."

Alex wondered if Magellan knew his good fortune.

"Then he isn't sleeping with you?"

"Not when I first go to bed, but by morning he's snuggled under the blankets. It just takes him awhile to get there."

Sheesh.

He'd definitely chosen the wrong topic if he'd hoped to keep his mind from going haywire again. Visions of Shannon in bed were a sure guarantee of heat and guilt and other emotions he didn't want to confront. Yet the guilt seemed further away now. Maybe he'd just needed to hear someone say that he'd made his wife happy. Kim's love hadn't been the selfish kind; she wouldn't want him to be alone.

And Kim *had* been happy. She'd made the most of their

time together, and found things that contented her when they weren't.

"How did the meeting go today?" Shannon murmured.

The ordinary "how was your day" question made Alex smile. "Great. It was about me being assigned grad students next term. They sound like a good bunch. And Rita—the pregnant student I told you about—came by and said she's decided to keep her baby. She still won't say who the father is, but at least her folks have calmed down and want to help."

"I should think they would," Shannon said indignantly. "That poor kid. Kane has a corporate program to keep young mothers in school, but it's easier when the parents are supportive. I'll give you the number for her to call."

"Thanks."

Rain continued to patter outside, and the swish-slosh of cars driving the wet streets came more often now that commuters were arriving home from the city. Everything was dark except for the lights twinkling on the Christmas tree, and Alex wished it was possible to freeze time.

Sitting there in the holiday warmth that Shannon had created, there wasn't any past or future, or any bad mistakes to repair or decisions to make. He could be like Magellan, exploring his way toward love and trust, nothing more to worry about than an unkind hand and sharply spoken words.

If only it were that easy.

Chapter Eleven

"**P**rooomise," pleaded Jeremy.

Shannon hesitated. Jeremy had asked her to be there when he woke up on Christmas morning, but that meant she would have to spend the night. It was one thing to sleep at the McKenzies' accidentally; it was another to do it deliberately.

"Yes. Promise?" Alex repeated his son's request. "You can sleep in Jeremy's room, and he can sleep with me."

What about Jeremy getting the wrong idea? She asked the question silently, and Alex shrugged. She would be returning to work after the New Year, so maybe he figured they would gradually see less and less of each other, that way letting Jeremy down lightly.

It was depressing, but she summoned a smile. "All right. Except I'll stay on the couch."

Alex frowned. The proposed sleeping arrangement probably didn't suit his notions of gallantry.

"Oh, pleeeze sleep in my room," Jeremy begged before his father could say something.

"Uh-uh, I want to be down here and see Santa coming down the chimney." She ignored the choking sound that came from Alex. "I never could catch him when I was little, but this might be the year I get lucky."

"Santa?" The youngster's face was scrunched up, doubtful but wanting to join in the fantasy at the same time.

"That's right. We'll put cookies and milk by the fireplace for him to eat, and leave the Christmas lights on all night."

"So he can find us?"

"Santa doesn't need lights to find us. He already knows you're a good boy."

"Daddy, I wanna sleep with Shannon and see Santa," Jeremy declared firmly.

Shannon clasped her hand over her mouth to keep from laughing as Alex sighed, long and hard. She now knew where Jeremy got his heartfelt sighs—from his daddy.

"Okay, you can sleep downstairs," Alex said, conceding defeat. "But Santa is hard to catch, so don't get your hopes up."

He received a spontaneous hug that nearly knocked him backward. "Goody. My daddy is the bestest daddy," Jeremy declared proudly.

That was one of the reasons parents made bad decisions, Alex decided wryly, so they could hear their kids saying they were great. Despite Shannon's chiding, he'd intended to stand firm on the subject of Santa Claus. The jolly old guy was merely a Christmas icon; his son needed to understand that it was the spirit of giving that was important.

Then Alex thought of the gifts for his family that he'd

shipped the day he'd met Shannon and realized the spirit of giving had little to do with his efforts. It was duty—the tired habit of sending gifts to people he hardly knew any longer.

What *had* he gotten for Gail?

He remembered. A gold chain. Something light for mailing to Japan. Probably similar to what he'd gotten the year before, and the year before that. Now he wished he had chosen something with more care.

"You *are* the bestest," Shannon said, smiling faintly. She rose and asked Jeremy to come with her into the den, so she could show him the computer games she'd brought.

How quickly she'd become a part of their daily lives. Now that it was the Christmas break and he didn't have to fight Jeremy over day-care, he ought to have begun the painful process of limiting their time together. But he hadn't been able to do it. The way his son's face lit up whenever he was around Shannon was too hard to resist.

After Christmas, Alex resolved.

He would break things off after the holidays. Shannon had restored the security his son had lost, and it must not be taken away too quickly.

What about *your* security?

Alex scowled at his nagging conscience. His next-door neighbor had become far too important to him, as well. She was so beautiful, it took his breath away, but that wasn't the problem. It was the way she made him believe in possibilities that truly disturbed him.

He'd believed Kim was the perfect woman for him, with her calm and gentle nature. Shannon was nothing like that, yet she was loving and generous and filled with the joy of living. Could she be his second chance?

* * *

"You push that button, and see what happens?"

Jeremy was all smiles as he played on Shannon's laptop. She'd ordered several games after he'd shown so much interest in computers at her office.

"You're spoiling him," Alex murmured when she walked into the kitchen. He gazed at her over the edge of his coffee cup, still blinking groggily, though he'd been awake for a couple of hours.

"They're educational games. I did my research. You can't spoil children with educational toys."

"Uh-huh."

She thought of the call she'd taken for Alex the previous day while he was out shopping, and smiled with secret delight. It had been Alex's sister, trying to reach him on his home phone. They'd introduced themselves and talked for a few minutes. Apparently Alex had called Gail a few days before, which started her thinking about coming to Seattle for Christmas. Hearing that, Shannon had instantly invited her to the O'Rourke holiday celebration. But because Gail still wasn't sure she'd been able to get a last-minute ticket for the nine-hour flight from Japan to Seattle, she'd asked Shannon not to tell Alex in case her travel plans fell through.

Shannon hoped Gail would be able to come. Families should be together for Christmas.

"I suppose you're grinning like a Cheshire cat because of that Santa Claus stuff," Alex grumbled.

"He's only four years old, not twenty-four. When did you stop believing?"

"I never believed."

Sadness filled Shannon at his flat tone. She'd been

raised by parents utterly devoted to each other and their children, who'd taught them about Irish mysticism and endless love, gifts she'd never fully appreciated before meeting Alex.

She'd fallen in love with him, the way her mother had fallen for a wild Irish lad. But it was by no means certain that Alex felt the same. He was so closed, so determined not to be disappointed again by love and life.

She'd thought her inability to be domestic was the biggest obstacle to love and marriage, but not with Alex. Those things faded into insignificance next to the big issues.

"Come on," she said suddenly. "Let's go someplace."

"Huh?"

"Jeremy?" she called. "We're going out." Shannon smiled at Alex. "It's December twenty-third and it has finally stopped raining. Let's celebrate."

She didn't want him to object; she wanted him to forget to frown and have fun. Grabbing his hands, she pulled.

"I'm twice your size," he said, beginning to smile.

With a neat twist of his wrists he tumbled her into his lap and laughed.

"The wrong idea," she reminded, but wanting very much to be kissed.

"Right." Alex's gaze lingered on her lips. "Little pitchers have big ears—and eyes."

Shannon pursed her mouth. "There's always the utility room," she suggested.

Apparently it was a suggestion he liked, because he swept her into the small dark room, slammed the door shut and cupped the back of her head. "I thought you'd hate being in here."

"I'm a woman. I change my mind easily."

That was all she got out, because Alex was kissing her so hungrily it was all she could do not to fall down. She felt him from her head to her toes and everywhere else between.

"J-just a friendly kiss," she managed to say when his hands travelled up her rib cage.

"You don't think this is friendly?" Alex's thumbs rotated over her nipples and she moaned.

"Daddy?" came a plaintive voice on the other side of the door. "Where are you an' Shannon?"

Alex uttered a single curse and Shannon grinned. "You bet it's friendly," she whispered. "But being *that* friendly is the way little pitchers get started in the first place."

Didn't he know it, Alex thought ruefully as Shannon eased free and opened the door.

"My goodness, Jeremy, you're all ready to go," he heard her exclaim. "You are growing up so fast. Let's go get my coat, too. I…um, think your daddy needs a couple of minutes to himself."

Alex took deep breaths and wished he was wearing loose sweatpants instead of jeans. When he could walk without cutting off his circulation, he followed Jeremy and Shannon into the living room. She looked at him with a merry expression.

"Feeling better?"

The little witch.

She knew exactly how aroused he'd been.

"Yes, I'm better. Where are we going?"

"I don't know. Malls. Toy stores. Chocolate shops."

"Yum," Jeremy crowed. "I like chocolate."

"So do I. Bet we can get your daddy to buy us a big chocolate Santa."

Alex was resigned as he followed Shannon and Jeremy

to the Jeep. A man could only fight the tide so long before getting pulled under, and Shannon was like the tide. An inexorable force sweeping through his life.

An ancient memory came to him of his father at the beach, solemnly explaining it was best not to fight a wave. If you got knocked over, go with it and then find your footing. A rare family vacation, beset by the usual arguments and recriminations, but in the middle was the remembrance of something good.

"Did you see him, Shannon?" Jeremy asked on Christmas morning as he danced around the living room in uncontained excitement. "Did you see Santa?"

Shannon shook her head. "Nope, I fell asleep like always."

"Me, too. But he came, didn't he?"

She looked at the packages around the tree. She'd put some of them there after Jeremy had drifted into slumber, but more had appeared. Alex must have sneaked down after they were *both* asleep.

"Yes, he came," Shannon said, a silly grin on her face. The last two days had been glorious, a wonderland of time spent with the man she loved to distraction, and a little boy who was as dear to her as if she'd given birth to him. She wouldn't let herself think about what would happen once the holidays were over. Not now, not until she had to.

"I gotta get Daddy." Jeremy went racing across the room, only to find his father on the staircase. "Santa came! *He came!* See, Daddy? An' he ate the cookies and drank all the milk."

"I see."

Alex sat on the steps, dressed in jeans and a sweatshirt—he was everything she'd ever wanted for Christmas.

The scent of coffee came from the kitchen, the machine's timer set by Alex the night before, but it was the empty plate of cookies that Shannon looked at. She'd forgotten to make it appear as if Santa had enjoyed his midnight treat. Alex had handled that little detail, and her heart swelled. Christmas was truly a miraculous time of year.

"Can we open presents now, Daddy?" Jeremy begged.

"Uh…okay." He still didn't look fully awake.

"Let your daddy have some coffee first." She went to the kitchen and poured a large cup. Alex accepted it with a smile and tugged her down next to him. She did wonder if he was thinking about Kim and wishing she was there, but Shannon couldn't resent the other woman's memory. Kim had loved her family, and was surely watching over them the way Shannon knew her father was watching over her, comforting her in dark times, and rejoicing in the good ones.

"Do you want cookies with that?" she asked softly, to keep Jeremy from hearing.

"Cookies?"

Her gaze flicked to the empty plate by the fireplace and back again. "Yes. Thanks for remembering. I was so sleepy, I wasn't thinking."

"I didn't eat anything. It must have been Santa."

"You…" Shannon laughed and leaned into the arm Alex put around her.

After a while he shook himself. "I think it's time to open presents," he said, and Jeremy clapped his hands.

Soon the living room was a sea of paper and ribbon, something that Magellan—who'd also been a McKenzie houseguest—enjoyed immensely, along with the cat toys Santa had left him. Shannon held her breath when Alex opened her gift, an old ship's sextant. He'd confessed a fascination with early sailing ships, but she couldn't be sure it was something he'd like.

"Shannon…it's extraordinary." He lifted the instrument from its velvet-lined case and checked the settings, peering through the eyepiece. "But you shouldn't have."

"I wanted to. And you should talk," she said, her fingers stroking the antique copper teakettle Alex had gotten to put by her fireplace. It was perfect. A little bit of Ireland, like her grandparents' home.

"This is from me, Shannon." Jeremy gave her a package and crawled into her lap. She had given him a telescope and books and other toys, but it was the picture of his mother that she'd sealed in a plastic key chain that he wouldn't put down.

"Thank you, Jeremy. It's darling—just like Magellan." It was a silver pin of a skittish cat, dancing on his toes.

He kissed her and sat looking at the picture of his mother. They had talked the night before, Shannon guessing that one of his wishes to Santa was that his mommy come home from heaven. Another was that he get a new mommy—Shannon.

The conflicting desires weren't troubling to a child Jeremy's age. She'd simply told him that Santa couldn't bring those kinds of gifts, but to remember that his mother wasn't any farther than his heart, and that grown-ups had to work things out for themselves.

"I'd better get ready to go," Shannon said after they'd bagged the paper and ribbons.

"We'll get ready, too," Alex promised.

He looked tense, she realized as she crossed to her condo carrying Magellan; she'd probably blown everything, asking him to have Christmas with the rest of the

O'Rourkes. She should have remembered he didn't have the best experiences with families. Yet surely it would be better once his sister arrived.

If she arrived, Shannon reminded herself. Gail McKenzie had sounded uncertain about her plans, saying only that she hoped to arrive on Christmas day from Japan and would prefer to rent a car rather than have anyone meet her. But it would be a great surprise gift if she did get there.

Alex bathed Jeremy and tried not to think about the way Shannon had looked when he'd gone downstairs to put Santa's packages beneath the tree. Angelic, her fiery nature muted by sleep. If Jeremy hadn't been dozing by the tree, he might have kissed her again.

"My son, the duenna," he muttered. A four-year-old chaperone.

"What's a dwayna?" Jeremy asked.

"It's just a word. You'll find out when you learn Spanish."

By the time they were both dressed and on their way next door, Shannon was already hauling boxes from her house and stacking them by the Jeep. "Why didn't you wait?" Alex asked, hurrying to help her.

"I didn't want to take longer than necessary."

He scowled, wanting to remind her that men had muscles to do the heavy work, yet knowing she'd just say something sassy and laugh at him. But he was particularly annoyed when he discovered one of the boxes was filled with bottles of sparkling grape juice, and another with sparkling cider. They really *were* heavy.

"Don't be mad," Shannon said winsomely, handing him a bag of gaily wrapped packages.

"I'm not mad…yes, I am. *Was* mad," he amended when

she smiled. Though she'd said to dress casually, she wore a soft, expensive-looking sweater and a velvet skirt that hugged her faithfully. The cat pin Jeremy had given her adorned her shoulder. Once they were in the Jeep, she hummed a Christmas tune as they headed for her mother's house.

It all seemed so *right*. Still, panic skirted the edges of Alex's consciousness. He didn't want to examine what he felt for Shannon. It was much easier dismissing his feelings as simple physical need and gratitude for what she'd done for Jeremy than acknowledging that something deeper and more complex had been growing since the day they'd met.

Shannon gave easy-to-follow directions and it wasn't long before they pulled into a tree-lined driveway. Alex didn't know what he'd expected to see, but the big old rambling house wasn't close. A porch wrapped around the house, and people spilled from the doors as they parked. It was the homiest place he could have imagined.

"Merry Christmas. You're late," cried a collection of voices, followed by hugs and exclamations of, "We missed you last night."

"What about last night?" he whispered in Shannon's ear when they stepped inside the front door. "Were you supposed to be here?"

She bit her lip. "The family usually has dinner and attends a candlelight service on Christmas Eve. I didn't have to go. We would have been welcome, but I figured…well…you know. And I didn't want to disappoint Jeremy."

Alex knew why Shannon hadn't said anything; she'd known he wouldn't want to attend the service.

"Goodness, is this Jeremy?" asked an older woman, who approached them with a warm smile.

Jeremy nodded, still clinging to Alex's hand, but he

looked intrigued by the color and laughter and happy chatter that filled the comfortable house. It was a new experience for both of them—like walking into a Norman Rockwell painting.

"My name is Pegeen," said the woman, introducing herself. "I'm Shannon's mother, and you must be Alex." Her Irish brogue had been softened but not erased by her years in America.

"I like Shannon," Jeremy declared before his father could say anything.

"So do I, darlin'. Do you want to meet my other grandchildren? The two oldest are close to your age. You'll enjoy playin' with them."

Jeremy readily released his grip on Alex's hand and followed Pegeen.

"I should have known," Alex murmured, shaking his head. It had been days since Jeremy had wanted Mr. Tibbles with him, and though Alex had put the rabbit in the Jeep as a precaution, it seemed apparent the stuffed animal wouldn't be needed.

"You should have known what?" Shannon asked.

"That your mother is a Pied Piper, just like you."

She grinned and drew him into the living room, introducing family as she went. The names became a blur of brothers and sisters, in-laws and children. And Kane O'Rourke, who held a small baby on his shoulder, was no longer the brisk executive or accusing brother, but a doting father. Meeting him that way, Alex would never have guessed he owned a multi-billion dollar corporation.

"Who's going to help bring everything in?" Shannon said, and though they complained, her five brothers donned coats and trooped out to the Jeep Cherokee.

"You always bring too much," Kane said when they were piling gifts near the Christmas tree, then carrying her contributions to the meal into the kitchen.

"But I didn't do it all. Alex, what is this about?" she asked, looking into several of the boxes.

"I had to contribute something and you wouldn't tell me what to bring."

An arm reached over Shannon's shoulder and took a can of cashews from the box she was examining. "Great, I'm starved."

"You're always hungry, Connor."

"Dinner isn't for hours."

With Alex distracted by her brothers Shannon took his coat and hung it with hers in the hall closet on the way to the kitchen. She wanted a word with her mother.

"Mom," she said, entering the kitchen.

"Yes, darlin'?"

"You do remember what I told you about Alex being just a friend, don't you? There's nothing going on between us." It wasn't quite a lie, but Shannon crossed her fingers nonetheless.

"He seems a fine young man."

"Yes, but what did you mean by asking Jeremy to meet your 'other' grandchildren? Like he's one of them?"

"A slip of the tongue, love."

Her mother never had slips of the tongue.

"Do *not* get carried away," Shannon warned. "Alex doesn't want to get married again. He has been very clear on the subject, so nothing is going to happen between us."

"Now, darlin', you can't blame me for bein' a bit hopeful. You've never brought a young man to dinner, much less

Christmas dinner. I haven't seen you so happy in a long while."

"He's a widower, Mom. It hasn't even been a year," Shannon said desperately. All she needed was to have her mother try some misplaced matchmaking. "*Please* don't say anything."

Pegeen touched her face. "I'll only say that I love you, dear. Now go on, and don't worry. It's Christmas."

Shannon hurried back to the living room and Alex made room for her on the couch. He was debating a point in football, and she rolled her eyes at how quickly the men had found a topic of common interest. There were times she felt like the odd person out in her own family. The women would congregate in the kitchen, talking about cooking and babies and other domestic interests, her brothers would talk sports or some other manly pursuit, and she didn't fit with either.

"How is that new kitten of yours doing?" asked Connor after several minutes. "Except for being skin and bones, he seemed to be healthy when I checked him."

"He's doing fine." She looked at Alex. "Connor has to endure the entire family bringing their animals to him for treatment."

"Like having a doctor in the family?"

"Something like that."

Alex nodded and wondered why he'd worried about coming to dinner at the O'Rourkes'. They were normal people, down-to-earth and thoroughly likable; no one would know they had access to inconceivable wealth. And Jeremy was having a ball, laughing and running around with two little girls who were as alike as two peas in a pod. His son was too young to think about the implications of having dinner with a woman's family, anyway.

Other O'Rourkes arrived, aunts and uncles and cousins whose names Alex didn't have a prayer of remembering. Children were hugged and given treats. Food was everywhere, snacks to hold everyone until the main event. Which, judging by the rich scents rolling from the kitchen, would be a feast of grand proportions.

Shannon divided most of her time between him and Jeremy, and Alex found himself missing her whenever she disappeared to chase after his son. It wasn't as if he'd barely seen her that day, or any other day in the past few weeks, and he didn't want to think about the implications.

"Try this," Shannon said, appearing after a particularly long absence.

He bit into the pecan and butter pastry. "It's great, but I'm not going to be able to eat dinner if you keep feeding me."

"Just be grateful she's not trying to cook dinner," joked Connor. "Or you'd need your stomach pumped."

Everyone laughed, and someone else added, "Or we'd be out on the street, waiting for the fire department to arrive."

"Hey, I only set fire to stoves, not houses," Shannon said lightly, but Alex saw her lips tighten. She left a couple of minutes later and he frowned, surprised her family didn't know she was bothered by their teasing.

He gave Connor a cold look. "If you had half the brains of your sister, you wouldn't say stupid things," he said, not caring if he sounded rude, or what they would think about him defending Shannon when it had obviously been a family joke.

He followed Shannon, grabbing both their coats when he saw her stepping out onto the front porch.

"Hey," he said, closing the door to shut out the prying ears of her family. "You're going to freeze out here."

"I'm tougher than I look."

Alex wrapped her in a coat. "Tough, right. You're shivering and turning blue. Why didn't you tell Connor and the others to stuff it?"

"Why should I? Everyone had a good laugh."

He caught her chin and made her look at him, frustrated by the way she guarded her deepest feelings. "*You* didn't enjoy it. You act like you don't care, but I know that isn't true, so don't pretend with me. Please, Shannon."

The remote expression in her eyes slowly vanished. "I'm used to the kidding. It's just that with you and Jeremy here…" She shrugged and rubbed her arms. "I mean, I explained we were just friends, so they don't have any reason to think it would embarrass me in front of you. But with families there's always this…I don't know…*thought* when someone new comes. An anticipation, wondering whether that person could be the 'one,' no matter what has been said."

Alex waited, trying to understand.

"New relationships are fragile and you have a son to think about. So having Connor joke around like that without thinking…it just…"

"Hurt?" Alex finished for her.

"Yes. He didn't know if we might really be involved, and if you'd get second thoughts about a woman who can't cook."

"Only an idiot would think that was important when it comes to you," Alex said adamantly.

Shannon tried to smile. "Don't get the wrong idea," she said. "My family is great, but all families have their moments."

"So, how long are you going to be mad at Connor?"

"Who said I was mad? My brothers can't help having the sensitivity of bricks. They've been handicapped from birth with the problem."

Alex laughed and hugged her close.

"You are the most amazing woman," he whispered in her hair. "I wish you could see yourself through my eyes, then you'd know what a miracle you are. If things were different…"

He stopped speaking, and pain lanced through Shannon. It meant so much to have Alex wanting to comfort her. She'd longed to find someone who would accept who she was. Yet now that she'd found the perfect man, he just wanted to be friends. But even that wouldn't last; they couldn't continue the dance between friendship and desire for much longer. It would tear them apart.

A light breeze ruffled the pine swag on the porch railings, and she thought ironically of the Christmas mistletoe her mother always hung above the front door.

She looked up.

Sure enough, it was there, tied in a bright red bow.

Alex looked, too, and shadows haunted his eyes. "Oh, Shannon, I wish—"

"No, don't talk about it. Let's pretend for one more day. It's Christmas."

"Yes, it is." Alex bent his head and his kiss, filled with passion and regret, brought tears to her tears, even as it sent streamers of fire through her blood.

When they were both gasping for breath, Alex released her. After a long minute regaining his composure, he looked over her head and lifted an eyebrow.

"It seems we have an audience. A very unhappy audience."

Shannon spun and saw three of her brothers. They were

glaring through the window at Alex as if he was a randy teenager groping their underage sister.

"Okay," she admitted grudgingly, "they have the sensitivity of bricks, but they're *protective* bricks."

Alex promptly burst out laughing.

Chapter Twelve

Shannon marched into the house, grabbed her eldest brother's arm, and dragged him into Pegeen's unoccupied sewing room. She slammed the door with a satisfying thud.

"What do you think you're doing?" she demanded.

"Nothing."

"Nothing my foot. How could you watch us through the window like that? It was none of your business."

"It most certainly *is* our business," he retorted. "You told Mom he didn't want to get married."

"I said he didn't want to get married *again*. He's a widower, with every right to make his own decisions. Besides, this isn't the eighteenth century. I can do what I want to do."

"I'm aware of that, but I don't want you getting hurt," Kane said quietly. *"Again."*

Shannon swallowed, shaken. She would have sworn the family knew little, if anything, about the times she'd had her heart broken.

"Alex is trying to survive," she whispered. "He's had too much happen, lost too much to risk it all again. Yes, I wish he'd change his mind, but he isn't responsible if I get hurt. I went into this knowing there wasn't a future."

"Ah, Shannon." Regret tinged Kane's voice. "Are you sure?"

"I've been able to fool myself a few times, but yes, I'm sure. So please let it alone. I want to spend Christmas with Alex and Jeremy, and for once not think about tomorrow."

She could tell he was reluctant, but he finally nodded. "All right. I'll tell Neil and Patrick to back off."

"Oh, no."

Shannon suddenly remembered she'd left Alex alone and sped out the door, Kane following close behind. She had visions of Alex and her other brothers rolling around on the living room floor, punching one another while the Christmas tree went flying in ten directions. Her brothers had primitive-level responses when it came to protecting the family. They became cavemen. Barely standing upright.

"How about playing some football later?" Neil said as she rushed into the room. He was standing with his arms crossed, practically nose-to-nose with Alex, who had assumed an equally aggressive stance.

"Yeah, football," agreed Patrick, a glint in his eyes that suggested he wouldn't mind tackling his sister's guest. In a purely friendly, I'm-gonna-kill-you way, of course.

"No football," Shannon said hastily.

"That's right." Kane stepped between the two men. "No contact sports. Shannon wouldn't like it."

"Is that right, Shannon?" Alex asked with a wink. He looked ready to laugh again, and she loved him even more for understanding that her brothers were a bunch of lovable lunatics. Considering what he'd told her about his parents' endless fighting, she would have expected him to grab Jeremy and march out at the first sign of dissent.

She turned to her four sisters-in-law. They were watching their husbands with a mixture of love and exasperation.

"Can't you control them?" she demanded.

Patrick's wife, Maddie, shifted the baby in her arms. "Nope. I'm afraid we're stuck with the bozos," she said cheerfully. "Let's have some hot cider."

The other women agreed and dragged their spouses into the dining room.

Alex tugged a length of Shannon's hair, seeing that she was still outraged. "Isn't this the point where you're supposed to tell me that they mean well, then assure me they're harmless?"

"They do and they are, and that's no excuse."

"But it's understandable." He knew why the O'Rourke brothers were hostile. They were a close-knit Irish family, with unshakable family values, and they saw him as a threat to their sister's happiness. It was a fascinating glimpse into a world he'd never seen before.

Shannon sighed finally and focused on him. "At least you're not running for the hills."

"I'm looking forward to dinner too much to run. Besides, I don't think I could drag Jeremy away from your nieces."

"He does seem to be having fun."

"Just like his daddy. Let's go have some of that cider."

Alex tucked Shannon's arm into his, and headed for the dining room. He *was* having fun. Food and laughter were a seductive combination—not as seductive as Shannon, but few things could compete with Shannon.

She had said they would eat around two in the afternoon. Alex wondered why it was planned for so late, then learned why when the family gathered around the Christmas tree, crowding into every possible corner as they opened packages.

Somehow, he wasn't surprised to find Jeremy and himself the recipient of several thoughtful gifts. There were a number that Shannon looked at, then put back under the tree, whispering instructions to her eldest brother who was playing Santa by reading labels and passing out packages. She seemed to be anticipating something, and when she heard a car turning into the driveway, she jumped to her feet.

"I hope this is another Christmas present," she said, touching Alex's shoulder before hurrying out to the foyer. When she returned, another woman stood behind her.

Alex froze.

"Everyone, this is Alex's sister, Gail," Shannon announced, drawing Gail forward. "She's here from Japan. Gail, this is everyone. Don't worry about anyone's name, just say 'hey you.'"

Gail.

Remembering their agonizing phone call of just a few days before, Alex felt his stomach clench. Gail looked tired and unsure of herself, but she smiled gamely at the huge, welcoming family. "I hope I'm not intruding."

"Nonsense," Pegeen said. "Come in, child, you look worn to a frazzle."

Alex belatedly rose and gave his sister an awkward kiss. "Jeremy," he said. "Do you remember your Aunt Gail?"

Jeremy didn't, but he'd been hugged so much that day, he was more than willing to get another. Soon he and Gail were sitting together, with Shannon pulling out the packages she'd set aside and giving them to the newcomer.

"Thank you…that's so thoughtful." Gail sounded overwhelmed, and Alex clenched his teeth. Shannon had obviously known his sister was coming, but why hadn't she told him?

After a while Gail seemed to relax, even joining with the O'Rourkes as they sang Christmas carols. Shannon shot him curious glances as she eased his sister into her family circle, the way she had done with him and Jeremy.

What could he say?

You should have told me that my sister, whom I barely know, is coming to Christmas dinner?

Yeah, that would really add to the spirit of the day.

Shannon knew something was wrong. Alex had hardly said two words during dinner, then shortly after his sister left for her hotel, turning down his offer to stay at the condo, he'd suggested they go home.

"Jeremy is already asleep," she murmured as he drove steadily through the darkness. Fog had crept over the Puget Sound area, but Christmas lights still glimmered in the murk.

"Yes."

"I think he had a good time."

"You know he did."

She expelled a breath. It was hard having a conversation with someone who was so tight-lipped. Had he taken a belated offense to her brothers' behavior? Or was it something else? She tried to think of anything else that might have disturbed him, but the worst offense of the day had been Patrick and Neil threatening his well-being in a game of tackle football.

At the condo Alex carried Jeremy upstairs and Shannon sank onto a chair in the living room, waiting for him to come down again. The holiday meal that had tasted so delicious only two hours before, now sat like lead in her stomach.

What had gone wrong?

When Alex returned, he didn't say a word, and she followed him into the kitchen. "I can't take the suspense any longer. What's wrong?"

"Nothing."

"I don't believe that."

"All right, I don't want to discuss it."

"Alex! Look at me. *What is wrong?*"

He threw his keys onto the counter, then turned to her, a fierce glare in his eyes. "Why didn't you tell me Gail was coming to Seattle? How did you even know she was coming?"

The question made Shannon's eyes widen. "She called you, one day while I was watching Jeremy. She wasn't sure she'd be able to get here, and because her plans weren't settled, she decided it was better to make her trip a surprise."

"You should have told me."

"It was what Gail wanted. For Pete's sake, Alex, she's your sister. I thought you'd be thrilled to see her."

"You don't know the score with my family," he retorted. "And you have no right to interfere. You should have discussed it with me before issuing invitations and keeping secrets. *You're not my wife.*"

"I know I'm not your wife," she said tightly. "And you've certainly made it clear that I'm never going to be. So why don't you take a flying leap and see where it takes you?"

Shannon spun, too angry to see straight. It didn't seem possible that Alex could be so awful. Even if he didn't know she was in love with him, he had to know she had strong feelings for both him and Jeremy.

"Where are you going?" he demanded.

"Home."

"I'll walk you over."

"Don't bother." She grabbed her purse and fished her keys from the outside pocket.

If it hadn't been for Jeremy, she would have slammed the door, but she remembered in time that he was asleep. He deserved a night of sugarplum dreams before he learned that his daddy was a confounded *jackass*.

Despite her refusal, Alex came outside and watched her walk the thirty feet to her own door safely. But it wasn't any comfort; it was just aggravating.

She had never *once* asked him to change his mind.

She'd tried to be a friend the way he wanted, and what had that gotten her?

Accusations and anger.

He was impossible.

But as she sank into a chair after letting herself into her condo, she remembered the tormented look in Alex's eyes. Tears streamed down her cheeks. Without even knowing what he was doing, he must have been looking for a way to break things off, a way to feel he was right about banishing her from his and Jeremy's life.

"Oh, Alex," she moaned.

She *could* be a good wife and mother, and still be herself. She finally understood there was more to making a home than being able to cook and clean. But their problems were about Alex's personal demons, not domestic responsibilities.

Alex had never had a family that was a haven, caring and supportive—even when they tried to interfere. Despite that, he had taken a chance by loving Kim, and he'd lost her. Shannon had wondered how many times a shattered heart could heal, and she was afraid Alex was beyond that limit. He was hurting, and there wasn't anything she could do about it.

"Meoowr?" Magellan cried and jumped onto her lap, looking at her anxiously.

"I'm afraid it's over, baby," she whispered.

He lapped a tear that had fallen onto her hand, then rested his chin on the spot.

Shannon looked around her home and realized there *was* something she could do to help Alex, but not with useless crying or reminding him of what they might have had together.

A strength she hadn't known she possessed filled her. She would call a Realtor first thing in the morning and list the condo for sale.

"Are you sure you can't stay longer?" Alex asked his sister as they waited for her plane to board.

"I wish I could, but I didn't plan this trip enough ahead of time." A light blush spread across Gail's cheeks. She had admitted to impulsively deciding to visit Seattle after his telephone call, only to be riddled with second thoughts of how he'd feel about seeing her.

"I'm glad you came," Alex said. He meant it, though he still winced when he thought of how he'd overreacted to Shannon's "surprise" two days before. Even at the time he'd known his response was hugely out of proportion. She hadn't interfered; her loving spirit simply couldn't imagine a sister being anything but a welcome visitor—especially not on Christmas day.

The O'Rourkes celebrated Christmas with all the excitement of small children, but they hadn't forgotten its meaning. Alex, who'd smugly told Shannon that he wanted his son to understand the spirit of giving, had lost its meaning completely.

The boarding call came and Alex hugged Gail close, only to find heat pricking his eyes. "You'll call," he said gruffly. "When you get in?"

"Of course."

"And if there's anything you need…*anything*, you let me know. We'll be on the next plane."

It didn't help his own composure when she gave him a watery smile. "Yes."

"Bye, Auntie Gail." Jeremy gave her a noisy kiss. "You promise to come see me again?"

"I promise."

Alex knew Gail would keep her promise. They had only begun talking, sorting out the tangle of their childhood, but it was a beginning that was long overdue. He and Jeremy would visit her in Japan, and Gail would come to Seattle. And in the meantime, they would force themselves past the awkwardness of talking on the phone, and find a way to be brother and sister, rather than strangers.

Thanks to Shannon.

The thought was uppermost on his mind during the drive home. Shannon had reshaped his life, and all he'd done was wound her, like all the other men who hadn't valued the remarkable woman inside that sophisticated package.

He wasn't ready to end things between them, no matter how often he'd thought it would be for the best. But what could he do to fix what had happened? Fixing relationships wasn't his forte; he was better at screwing them up.

When Alex turned into their shared driveway, he braked to an abrupt halt.

A For Sale sign stood on Shannon's lawn.

He cursed.

"You said a bad word, Daddy," Jeremy said placidly. "Can we go see Shannon? I miss her a whole bunch."

They were going to see Shannon, all right. He was going to find out why she was leaving without even telling him. Jeez, one little fight and she was bailing out.

"Stay here, Jeremy. I'll see if she's home." Alex left the heat running in the Jeep, then stormed up to Shannon's door. He pounded on it furiously. "Shannon, what in hell is going on?"

It opened abruptly and he scowled when she didn't say anything right away.

"Explain that." He pointed to the Realtor's sign.

"Where is Jeremy?" she asked instead. He wanted to shake her.

"Jeremy is in the Jeep, keeping warm." Alex looked at her hungrily, aching at the dark smudges beneath her eyes. "I don't understand. I was a jerk the other night, but that's hardly a reason to do something so drastic. Can't you just blame it on faulty male chromosomes?"

"It isn't that simple. I really can't—"

"I just want an explanation," he shouted, not caring who heard him, or what they'd think. That was what Shannon had done; she had finally made him as nuts as the insane people he'd grown up wanting to escape. "Please explain," he said more quietly. "*Please,* Shannon."

"I...I know that it's hurting you, me being here."

"It isn't that bad," he said, his throat tight from everything he wanted to say, but couldn't.

"Yes, it is. We're tearing each other apart. We can't keep living next to each other, and since I don't have a child to think about, it's only right that I'm the one to leave."

Alex stared. The stark unhappiness in Shannon's eyes wasn't about wounded feelings. She loved him, with more intensity and goodness than he could ever deserve.

Memories flitted through his head: raging battles between his parents, the big and small cruelties they'd handed out on a daily basis. They'd loved each other, too, before it turned to hatred. But he finally knew why they could hurt each other so badly...it was because they'd cared more about their own concerns and well-being than about each other.

But Shannon cared about him.

She cared so much, she was willing to put him and his son's welfare ahead of her own. She would never intentionally use his heart against him. All he had to do was find the courage to risk losing everything again.

And to gain everything.

Because he already loved her. She'd become more important to him than breathing, though he had done his best to deny the truth and push her away because of fear and guilt.

"I love you," he breathed, suddenly free in a way he'd never been. The decision was really very simple—life might be uncertain, but without Shannon, it wasn't worth living. "I know I was a fool, but don't leave us. Jeremy and I can't make it without you."

"You can't...it's too soon."

Alex put her hand over his heart, pressing her fingers to its beating rhythm.

"You're wrong, Shannon. You were just in time. All my

life I've been afraid of emotions because of my parents' mistakes. I married a woman I loved, but I let my childhood keep us from the closeness we should have had."

Shannon watched him doubtfully.

"I don't want to make that same mistake twice," he said urgently. "You showed me that hiding from what I feel isn't really being alive, and I want to be alive. But can you trust me enough to share all the things you've kept hidden since your father died?"

Shannon trembled. She'd expected Alex to be relieved she was leaving: expected that he would allow a polite good-bye to Jeremy and be glad he didn't have to deal with her any longer. Yet now he was offering her the world.

"I…are you sure?"

"More sure than I've ever been. Please marry me, Shannon. Love me forever. Trust me enough to be strong for you when things are bad."

Shannon searched Alex's face and saw unqualified adoration. Love and trust and a thousand other promises were vowed in his level gaze.

"I've never spoken about my father with anyone, not the way I talked to you about him," she said softly. "Or of most of the things I've told you about, and it wouldn't have happened if I didn't trust you already." Alex's heart pounded furiously beneath her fingers. "But as much as I trust you, I love you even more," she finished.

He pulled her close and she laughed.

"Jeremy can see us. What if he gets ideas?"

"My son had the right idea all along. But come on, let's tell him."

She laughed again as she was rushed across the lawn to the Jeep Cherokee.

"Good news, Jeremy," Alex said exultantly. "We have a late Christmas present for you."

"What is it?" Jeremy asked, wriggling impatiently as his father released him from the car seat.

"Shannon is going to be your new mommy."

Jeremy became very still. "For honest real, Daddy?"

"For honest real, son."

Jeremy lunged into Shannon's arms. "I was afraid, but on Christmas, my first mommy told me it would be okay," he said, his voice muffled against her shoulder. "She sang me a song and said Daddy just needed to let go. I didn't know what that meant, but she said Daddy knew."

Shannon blinked away tears, though she didn't know how Alex would react to his son's declaration. She'd always accepted there was a larger world beyond human perception, but Alex had never been taught that love didn't know any boundaries.

"Then it's unanimous," Alex said, smiling as if he'd never stop. "Trust me," he whispered.

She nodded and he gathered them both into his arms. Their lips met in a kiss that drove away the last shadows and doubts, everything but the miracle of two people finding each other.

Epilogue

"**D**id you convince her?" Alex demanded as his wife put down the phone.

"I talked to her, that's all," Shannon said. "You know Gail has to make up her own mind, and it won't help if you pressure her one way or the other."

"But her firm is opening a division in the Seattle area," Alex fumed. He'd become much closer to his sister in the past year and wanted them to spend more time together. "And if she lived here, then she wouldn't have to miss Christmas with us because of some idiotic project."

Shannon laughed and rubbed the small of her back. She loved being pregnant, but the baby's size was beginning to interfere with daily activities…like getting dressed and climbing the two staircases of their 1890 farmhouse.

She sighed with pleasure as she looked around the living room. It was the last sort of house she'd wanted to live in again, but she'd changed her mind the moment they'd seen it and Alex had gotten a kid-in-a-candy-shop look on his face. The old place was great to decorate for Christmas…something she'd actually managed to do on her own.

Of course, she might have gone overboard. With the lighted pine garland on the staircases and fireplace mantels, dozens of poinsettias, and Christmas trees in every window, it was a holiday wonderland. Kane had insisted she take maternity leave early, so she had used the time to decorate to her heart's content.

She had also come up with the idea of having several cookie-baking parties at the house, so Jeremy's cookie cravings had been handled by his new aunts and his grandmother—no fire extinguishers needed.

"Are you all right?" Alex fussed as he pushed pillows behind her back. "You need to rest more."

"I'm fine. If I didn't know better, I would think you'd never gone through this before. But I do know better, because the proof is attending kindergarten this year."

"It's the first time I've gone through it with *you*," he retorted. "And you're so damned uncooperative about following the doctor's orders, you're making me crazy."

Shannon grinned. "She said to put my feet up several times a day, not to become an invalid."

"She also said not to get too tired."

"You're the one getting tired, running around and waiting on me. It's your Christmas break. You have to quit—" Her scolding was smothered by Alex's kiss, which started out teasing, and ended with them both out of breath.

"Have I told you today how much I love you?" he whispered.

"Yes, but I never get tired of hearing it," she murmured. The past year had seen them through a family wedding, fierce disagreements, home-selling and buying, and the kind of passionate loving that made her current condition all the sweeter. Things hadn't been easy, they'd both needed to make adjustments and compromises, but Shannon hadn't expected easy. Anybody could have easy; she wanted something worth working to have and to keep.

"Jingle Bells, Jingle Bells," sang Jeremy as he trotted into the room. He was a year bigger, and even dearer to Shannon's heart, if that was possible. A few months before, he had given Mr. Tibbles to her for permanent safekeeping, and she'd carefully packed the tired rabbit away with the baby clothes that Kim McKenzie had saved. "Mommy, when are we gonna go singing?"

Alex raised an eyebrow at his wife and tried to look stern. "Singing? In your condition?"

"It's Christmas Eve." She smiled innocently. "I thought everyone could go caroling before we attend the candle-lighting service. Jeremy has never gone caroling before, so it's an educational experience. Besides, he'll have fun."

By "everyone" Alex knew she meant the entire O'Rourke clan. Little by little, Shannon had given him her family, pulling Gail into their circle of love, as well. She'd been making noises about his brother lately, and Alex knew as soon as Sam emerged from his research assignment in the Arctic, he'd be overwhelmed by his sister-in-law.

Alex grinned.

Sam didn't stand a chance against a determined redhead. None of the McKenzies did. To Alex's never-ending amazement, he actually enjoyed the inevitable battle of wills between him and his wife, knowing that love hovered as an ever-present peacemaker.

"Am I gonna have a new brother or sister for Christmas?" Jeremy asked, eyeing Shannon's nonexistent lap. He had to be content with sitting next to her on the couch.

"Santa is working on that," Shannon said, squirming in an attempt to get comfortable.

Alex felt a familiar anxiety. The baby was already overdue. He wanted to suggest that they stay home where it was warm and dry and quiet, but knew his wife would laugh and say that he worried too much. It was hard to believe how much she'd changed his life, opening his mind and heart, refusing to back down on anything she thought was right and important.

As the afternoon and evening progressed, he tried to push the worry to the back of his mind. And, amid the peace of the candlelighting service to celebrate the birth of another small baby, he breathed a prayer of thankfulness and hope for the future.

When Shannon opened her eyes on Christmas morning, she decided she must be in heaven. Magellan—now a magnificent adult-size cat—purred contentedly at the foot of the bed. Small flickers of flame still danced in the bedroom hearth. And her husband held her close, his warmth stretching from the back of her head to her heels, while his hand rested carefully on her rounded tummy.

Alex still didn't like waking up, but that was okay. Shannon knew how to make him smile, even if it *was* morning.

She grimaced at the persistent ache in her back. Correction: she could make him smile when she *wasn't* nine months pregnant and ready to pop at any moment. Seducing her sleeping husband wasn't a problem when she could do more than just *think* about it.

"Mommy, Daddy, Santa came again," Jeremy shouted,

bursting through the door. "An' he ate all the cookies and drank the milk. He even lef' me a card. See? I can read the words. It says Thank you."

Jeremy dropped the card on the bed and went tearing down the stairs again.

Shannon smiled.

"Nice touch," Alex murmured behind her.

One of her eyebrows lifted. "Don't look at me. I didn't leave a card—you're the one who ate the cookies and milk."

"I thought you ate them."

Shannon squirmed awkwardly to face him. "Not a bite."

They looked at each other, then they shook their heads. Some mysteries were better left unanswered, though Shannon privately thought Alex was pulling her leg. He loved teasing her about "Santa," declaring she probably still believed in the jolly old fat guy.

Maybe.

She'd never received a greater gift than her family, both the one she'd been born into, and the one given to her only a year before. If Santa truly represented the spirit of love and generosity, then she believed in him wholeheartedly.

After their own celebration around the living-room Christmas tree, they drove to her mother's house, with Jeremy singing his new favorite song, "Silent Night."

"It's an improvement on Jingle Bells, but he's still off-key," Alex murmured after they arrived and Jeremy went tearing across the yard to leap into his Uncle Kane's arms.

Shannon patted Alex's hand. "That's okay, honey, he gets his singing ability from you."

A mock glare was followed by a kiss as he lifted her from the high seat of the Jeep. "Are you sure you shouldn't be home in bed?" he asked.

"Positive." Shannon kissed his nose, but she was grateful for his strong arm as they climbed the porch steps. She hadn't told him about the contractions she'd felt before leaving their house. They were barely noticeable, and she wanted them to enjoy Christmas before making a mad dash to the hospital. Of course, O'Rourke babies had a habit of appearing at the most inopportune moments, and she figured this one wouldn't be any different.

"Surprise," Pegeen said as she pulled Gail out from behind the Christmas tree. "Look who flew into Seattle this morning."

"You said you couldn't come," Alex exclaimed as he embraced his sister.

"I didn't want to disappoint you if I had to cancel." Gail hugged her nephew as he launched himself at her. She smiled at Shannon and gave her a kiss over Jeremy's head. "Pegeen helped to arrange it."

"Now, none of that. I said you're to call me Mom, like all my other children," Pegeen scolded.

Alex saw the pleased blush on Gail's cheeks and felt regret for everything his own parents had missed over the years. But as Shannon snuggled next to him on the couch, he decided that Christmas wasn't a time for regret; it was a time for counting blessings.

Like the Christmas before, there was food and laughter, eggnog and hot cider to drink. Jeremy played with his cousins, and babies were passed from one welcoming arm to another.

Before dinner, Shannon went into the kitchen and sat in a chair, watching the bustle. She no longer felt left out because she didn't cook or do things like the other women in the family; she was truly Jeremy's mother and a passionately loved wife, and those were the only things that counted.

But Pegeen's sharp gaze wasn't to be discounted, and after a few minutes she leaned over her pregnant daughter. "How far apart, darlin'?"

Shannon laughed and shook her head. "I should have known you'd guess. The contractions are over thirty minutes apart, and my water hasn't broken yet, so there's plenty of time."

"Hmmm. 'Tis a good thing your cousin, Liam, is here."

Liam O'Rourke was a doctor, but Shannon had every intention of having her baby at the hospital, or her husband would never let her hear the end of it.

"I'll be fine," she said. "You had nine babies. You should find this stuff old hat. Positively boring."

"Never. And to think we'll have a Christmas babe…" Pegeen gave a happy sigh. "'Tis even better than I'd hoped."

"Bet you never thought I'd be next," Shannon said, smiling as she patted her drum-tight tummy.

"You're wrong." Pegeen kissed her daughter's forehead. "I knew when I met Alex and saw the way he looked at you. A fine man denyin' his own heart, but lovin' you with all of it, just the same."

Much later, as Shannon sat with Alex's fingers intertwined with her own, she knew they couldn't wait any longer. She'd managed to slip out of the room whenever a contraction was coming so he wouldn't guess, but something told her it was time.

"Um…Alex?" she murmured.

"Yes, darling?"

"I think it's time to get the Jeep warmed up."

"Are you…" He took one look at her face and leapt to his feet. *"Oh, my God, the baby's coming!"*

She laughed through the pain gripping her abdomen. "Well, it's not coming this minute, but let's not wait too long."

Liam was at her side in an instant, asking questions and taking her pulse. When Alex raced back into the room, her cousin calmly assured him they had plenty of time.

While everyone talked, assuring them Jeremy would be taken care of, Shannon donned her coat. She wanted to walk out under her own steam, but her husband would hear none of it. He carried her outside and in the glittering illumination of Christmas lights she saw excitement and worry on his handsome face.

"We'll be fine," she said as he put her in the passenger's seat. "Babies have been getting born since the beginning of time." But Shannon knew he would worry just the same.

They were met at the hospital by an efficient contingent of medical personnel, including her own obstetrician. Liam had come, as well, and the two doctors consulted as she was prepped.

An hour passed, then another, with Alex holding her hand and counting the way they'd practiced in childbirthing class. Her water broke late, and then everything happened in a rush. Twenty minutes later, she delivered a healthy, six-pound-nine-ounce daughter.

The nurse went out to the waiting room, where Gail McKenzie and the O'Rourkes had crowded together in anticipation. A happy roar burst out at the announcement, discernable even from the delivery room. Jeremy's excited cries rose above the rest; he'd gotten a sister for Christmas and it seemed to be exactly what he'd wished.

Later in her room, Shannon drowsily watched as Alex sat by the bed and gazed at their little girl, awe and adoration in his face. They had counted fingers and toes together, marveling at her dark red hair and angelic face, but this was her daddy's time; a time for silent promises and hopes for the future.

Tears pricked her eyes and Shannon knew that tonight, of all the nights in her life, she missed her own father the most. Yet even as the thought formed, she heard echoes of Keenan O'Rourke's voice in her mind and heart, and knew that he was watching and rejoicing.

Alex tore his gaze from the sleeping baby. "What is it?" he asked, knowing instantly that the darkness in his wife's eyes didn't come from discomfort or exhaustion.

"I was just thinking about my father...wishing he could be here."

"He *is* here, Shannon. Nothing could keep him away."

"I know." She smiled and held out her hand. "I've been thinking...we've talked about so many names, but maybe we should consider using Kimberly."

Alex swallowed, trying to control the lump in his throat. Shannon accepted the life he'd once shared with Kim; she even celebrated that life because of her love for Jeremy. Few women could have been so generous.

"I think you're wonderful," he said when he could talk. He looked down at the precious bundle he held, the tiny infant who already possessed his heart and soul as completely as her mother did. "But I can't think of a better name than Holly Noel for a little girl born on Christmas."

"Oh...all right."

Shannon's radiant smile filled Alex and he leaned forward.

"I love you, Shannon McKenzie," he whispered against her lips, and heard it returned with sweet promise.

Sometimes the greatest miracles of all were the ones you never knew you needed.

* * * * *

SILHOUETTE *Romance*®

Matilda Grant signed on to a reality
show to win fifty thousand dollars,
but once she met contestant
David Simpson all the rules changed!

Don't miss a moment of

The Dating Game

by

SHIRLEY JUMP

Silhouette Romance #1795

**On sale
December 2005!**

Only from Silhouette Books!

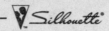

SPECIAL EDITION™

Here comes the bride...
matchmaking down the aisle!

HIS MOTHER'S WEDDING
by Judy Duarte

When private investigator Rico Garcia
arrived to visit his recently engaged
mother, the last thing on his mind was
becoming involved with her
wedding planner.

But his matchmaker of a mom
had other ideas!

*Available January
wherever you buy books.*

Where love comes alive™

If you enjoyed what you just read,
then we've got an offer you can't resist!

Take 2 bestselling love stories FREE!

Plus get a FREE surprise gift!

Clip this page and mail it to Silhouette Reader Service™

IN U.S.A.	IN CANADA
3010 Walden Ave.	P.O. Box 609
P.O. Box 1867	Fort Erie, Ontario
Buffalo, N.Y. 14240-1867	L2A 5X3

YES! Please send me 2 free Silhouette Romance® novels and my free surprise gift. After receiving them, if I don't wish to receive anymore, I can return the shipping statement marked cancel. If I don't cancel, I will receive 4 brand-new novels every month, before they're available in stores! In the U.S.A., bill me at the bargain price of $3.57 plus 25¢ shipping and handling per book and applicable sales tax, if any*. In Canada, bill me at the bargain price of $4.05 plus 25¢ shipping and handling per book and applicable taxes**. That's the complete price and a savings of at least 10% off the cover prices—what a great deal! I understand that accepting the 2 free books and gift places me under no obligation ever to buy any books. I can always return a shipment and cancel at any time. Even if I never buy another book from Silhouette, the 2 free books and gift are mine to keep forever.

210 SDN DZ7L
310 SDN DZ7M

Name	(PLEASE PRINT)	
Address	Apt.#	
City	State/Prov.	Zip/Postal Code

Not valid to current Silhouette Romance® subscribers.

Want to try two free books from another series?
Call 1-800-873-8635 or visit www.morefreebooks.com.

* Terms and prices subject to change without notice. Sales tax applicable in N.Y.
** Canadian residents will be charged applicable provincial taxes and GST.
  All orders subject to approval. Offer limited to one per household.
  ® are registered trademarks owned and used by the trademark owner and or its licensee.

SROM04R   ©2004 Harlequin Enterprises Limited

SILHOUETTE *Romance*®

COMING NEXT MONTH

#1798 LOVE'S NINE LIVES—Cara Colter and Cassidy Caron
PerPETually Yours
Justin West wasn't looking for commitment, but everything about
Bridget Daisy exemplified commitment—especially her large
tabby cat, who seemed to think there was room for only one
male in Bridget's life. Justin couldn't agree more. So he vowed
to be a perfect gentleman. Only problem was he had *never* been
a gentleman....

#1799 THAT TOUCH OF PINK—Teresa Southwick
Buy-a-Guy
Uncertain how to help her daughter win a wilderness survival badge,
Abby Walsh buys ex-soldier Riley Dixon at a charity bachelor
auction. But will their camping trip earn Abby's *romantic* survival
skills merely a badge for courage, or a family man to keep?

#1800 SOMETIMES WHEN WE KISS—Linda Goodnight
Family business might have brought Jackson Kane home after
ten long years but it had always been personal between him and
Shannon Wyoming. Now he was her key to holding on to all that
she held most dear...but what price would she pay for saying
"yes" to his proposal?

#1801 THE RANCHER'S REDEMPTION—Elise Mayr
Desperate to save her sick daughter, widow Kaya Cunningham had no
choice but to return to the Diamond C Ranch and throw herself on the
mercy of her brother-in-law. And though Joshua had every reason to
despise Kaya for the secret she'd kept from his family, his eyes reflected
an entirely different emotion....